The Magical Adventures of...

HENRY OWL

The Tyrannosaurus Rex : The Honey Thief : The Ivory Hunters

By Nick Wadham

Illustrated by Maddy Cook

Typeset by Jonathan Downes,
Cover and Layout by SPiderKaT for CFZ Communications
Using Microsoft Word 2000, Microsoft Publisher 2000, Adobe Photoshop CS.

First published in Great Britain by CFZ Press

CFZ Press
Myrtle Cottage
Woolsery
Bideford
North Devon
EX39 5QR

© CFZ MMXIV

ISBN: 978-1-909488-19-9

For Amy Beatrice and
Thea Rose.
Be Wild and Daddy!

For my son Henry:
But for whom the Owl wouldn't have a name

I hope you enjoy Henry's
adventures

Nick Wodhem

X

Henry Owl and the Tyrannosaurus Rex

Chapter One
The Tooth

 enry Owl is a young Snowy Owl (he is eight – in owl years), and today he woke up very excited! Today he was going to the seaside with Mummy Owl, Daddy Owl, Lily and Harriet Owl (his older sisters).

After a long hot fly in the summer sun they arrived.

Poor Daddy Owl was red faced and puffing because he had to carry all of the heavy picnic stuff!

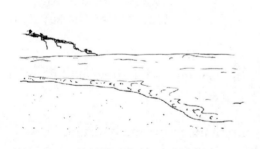

The beach looked white, shiny and soft, the sea was sparkling; it was as blue as the sky with small gentle waves that whispered across the shore and fizzled away as they kissed the sand.

"This is going to be great!" thought Henry as he dashed towards the sea.

"Hold on Henry!" called Mummy Owl. "You have to help carry the buckets and spades first! *Then,* you can run off and play with your sisters when we have the blanket set up."

"Oh, mum, they're boring, all they want to do is giggle at the boy owls; do I really have to play with them?"

Mummy Owl smiled kindly at Henry.

"Of course not, you can play on your own if you like."

With the buckets set, and the beach blankets laid, Henry was off to explore. At the top of the beach there were cracked and jagged cliffs:

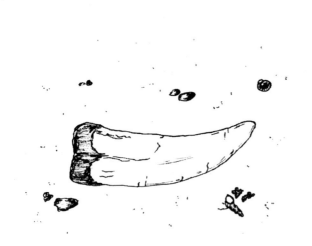

some of them had just fallen down after a bad sea storm. Henry climbed around on the big rocks, pretending to be an explorer, looking for lost pirate owl treasure. Then, something caught his eye, something white and long, pointed at one end, curved, and, yes! It was a tooth! A huge tooth! Dare he say it? A dinosaur tooth!

With his find firmly clutched in his wing he half flew, half flapped his way back to where his parents were sitting.

His heart pounding, he drew up to his mum and dad, and in between frantic breaths he gleefully announced his discovery – his face alight with excitement.

"Look at...what I've...found, it's a...dinosaur tooth!"

Breathlessly he handed it to his dad, who gave Henry's tooth the due attention it deserved; he raised a brow.

"Hmm, yes, without a doubt, I bet it's a big meat-eating dinosaur. Just look at the sharp edges! It looks like it fell out yesterday," he continued in a teasing, jokey fashion. "Better make sure the owner isn't anywhere nearby."

"Dad!" groaned Henry.

His mum was just as appreciative, but all his sisters did was to tell him to get a life. Girls: so boring! They would be interested all right if it was a picture of Johnowlthan Depp, or Owlando Bloom!

Forgetting the girls, he went back to the cliff-fall where he had found the tooth.

As he wandered, he noticed something rather peculiar indeed. When he was facing a certain way, the tooth in his wing tip began to buzz and rumble about! The longer he walked, the stronger it got, until he saw the great big black cave.

He checked. No one else seemed to have noticed it. Standing with his back to the sun, the cave certainly did not look much fun.

The tooth sent a tingle of adventure through him. It started at his wing tip and ended up making his heart beat faster. What an adventure it would be to explore the cave!

Heaving in a deep breath he stepped in. Nothing happened. All he could hear was the dripping of water, plipping and echoing around the solid walls, in imitation of the clicking of his claws on the ground-rock. It smelt of stale seaweed and slime. He walked further into the dreary gloom. Then, the tooth began to glow! This time he had no doubt that magic was happening! He almost tripped up on a big boulder.

But, it was not a boulder; it was a huge skull. A huge skull that was connected to a huge skeleton.

There was a tooth missing from the skull.

Henry brought his one closer to see if it was the one that had fallen out. He slid it in. A perfect fit. When he tried to take it back out, it was stuck. The skull moved!

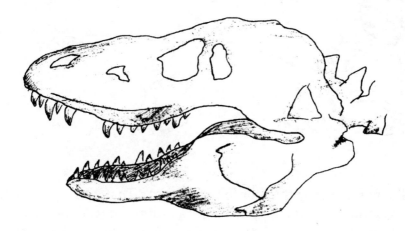

With a squeak, Henry jumped back, he tripped and plopped down on his bottom in a big puddle. Splash! But he did not notice the cold as the big skull began to rise. Its mouth opened and showed all of the teeth. They looked like a row of very scary bread knives. Henry was terrified! The huge head let out an enormous yawn.

"Oh, that's better," it said. Then it noticed Henry sat in front of it.

"Hmm, and what do we have here?" it asked in a deep voice.

"Please don't eat me!" Henry Owl shrieked.

"Eat you! Oh my, I don't even know what you are," the dinosaur thrust its head right up to Henry. "You might be poisonous!"

"I'm not..." Henry thought for a moment. "That's right, I'm very poisonous, and if you eat me you will get a tummy ache. I'm an owl."

The huge skeleton pushed itself up as far as it could, clicking like a bundle of sticks and looked down at Henry. Its eye sockets were big enough to put big beach balls in. Henry was sure his dad would fit in one of them quite easily.

"An owl you say. I've never seen a dinosaur that looked like you before. Have you evolved recently?"

Henry was confused.

"Have I what?"

"Evolved, my boy."

"No - what's immould?"

If the dinosaur had a face, by now it would have been smiling kindly, but it showed in its deep chuckle.

"No - ee-vole-ve." it said patiently.

Henry thought about the word. He had heard about it at school, but could not quite remember it, or what it meant.

"I don't think so. What does evolve mean?" he asked.

"It means when an animal changes very slowly over thousands and millions of years. It helps them to survive when the world changes."

"No.' Henry replied. 'I'm only eight and three quarters."

The dinosaur changed its line of questioning.

"What's your name, little owl?"

"My name's Henry Owl, and I'm not a Little Owl, I'm a Snowy Owl. What's your name?"

"My name is Toothy. I'm a *Tyrannosaurus rex*," replied the huge monster in a serious voice that somehow sounded sad. "And I'm a long way from home."

The dinosaur hung his head in despair.

"Don't be sad, Toothy," Henry said, trying to comfort him. "I'll help you find your way. There's magic in here and I think we can use it to get you home."

"How do you know?" asked Toothy.

"Because I felt it when I had hold of your tooth, I think you are magic, Toothy."

"Me?" asked Toothy in surprise.

"Yes, so take my wing and let's find out."

Toothy did as he was told. Henry felt the tingling feeling again, but this time it was much stronger. They felt the floor start

to spin around, the cave walls were blurring and streaks of light started to flash by like lasers.

The next thing Henry knew was that instead of being in a cave, they were in a hot and humid jungle clearing. Henry's face was plastered with amazement.

"Wow, where are we?"

"We are in the same place," Toothy replied, casually. "Only now, it is seventy million years before you were born."

Henry Owl just could not believe it. He looked at all the giant plants around him. The sun shone hot in the sky and glowed through the big green leaves of the giant fern trees; he saw huge bird things flying high above him.

"Look at those giant birds; they must be ten feet across!" he exclaimed.

"Oh, those aren't birds, and never will be. They are Pterosaurs." He pointed over to some two legged creatures in the bushes. "But those are theropods; your great great grandparents millions of times over."

"There a pods? What's there a pod?"

Toothy let slip a smile of patience and kindness. "Theh - row - pods. They will become birds in time. That one is a raptor. Look see? It has feathers and a beak. One day there will be a terrible film about them that gets it all wrong." Henry's face contorted as he tried to say the complicated word as they moved on.

"Look at you, Toothy! You are all covered in skin again," Henry pointed.

15

There was a small pool of water nearby and Toothy looked into it. His huge face was beaming a smile from ear to ear. Well, where Henry imagined Toothy's ears would be if he had them. Instead there was a big hole on each side of his head to let sound in. Toothy's skin was magnificent. It was covered in enormous scales and richly textured lumps and bumps, all different greens and browns. Toothy looked like he had stripey and leafy patterns all over him.

His eyes were enormous, yellow and had black slits for pupils. If Toothy were not Henry's friend, he would be very scary indeed.

In a green flash, something flew into the clearing. It was a flying lizard, the size of a crow. As quick as lightning, Toothy swung his head towards it and snapped it out of the air and swallowed it whole. Henry

Owl's eyes widened with shock.

"Why did you do that?" he asked, suddenly a little bit afraid.

"Do what, Henry?" Toothy was puzzled.

"Eat that little flying dinosaur. Aren't you all supposed to be friends?"

"Well, I'm hungry, I can't help it. I'm a *Tyrannosaurus rex*, it's what I do; I eat other dinosaurs. What do you eat?"

Henry hesitated before he answered.

"Um, I eat mice and voles."

"And what are they?" probed Toothy.

"Animals," replied Henry Owl, meekly.

"Well, there we are then, we both eat other animals," Toothy smiled.

"Shall we be friends?" asked the dinosaur, after a second of thought.

Henry Owl thought to himself. Can an eight-year-old owl and a seventy-million-year-old *Tyranosaurus rex* be friends? One of his sisters was friends with a lumpy toad, so he saw no reason why not. Henry smiled.

"Okay," he said.

"Right, Henry, why don't you flap on up here and sit on my head? Then I can take you to where I live and you can meet my family."

Chapter 2
The Missing Eggs

enry was clinging on very tightly with his sharp claws. He was worried he might hurt Toothy, but Toothy's bumpy scaly skin was so strong he didn't notice. As they ran, Henry realised that each of Toothy's strides must have been at least fifteen feet apart; the trees were going past quite fast, possibly twenty five miles per hour. Stomp, stomp, stomp, went Toothy's huge feet,.

Henry noticed that Toothy ran on his toes, not the whole of his feet; he left foot prints that were about a foot long, but the whole of his foot was easily one metre in length. They passed lots of other dinosaurs as they raced to Toothy's family.

All of them ran away, screaming for their lives and as a warning to anyone else who may be nearby.

"Run for your lives, Toothy's back!"

Some of the dinosaurs were quite large and Henry wondered why they were running away too, and why they were so scared of him. Toothy explained that during the Late Cretaceous Period, he was the top predator, and how most of the other dinosaurs would end up on his dinner table if they were not quick enough to get out of the way. He was in the middle of explaining all of this when he skidded to an abrupt halt.

"What's the matter Toothy, are we there yet?"

"No we're not, but we do have a problem."

In his haste to get home Toothy had failed to notice the colossal object on the path in front. Henry looked ahead and saw an odd looking dinosaur facing them, it was about ten feet tall and thirty feet long, it had a strange looking head with two large forward pointing horns, and a smaller one above what looked like a sharp beak. It had a funny looking frill at the back of its head that seemed to protect its neck. It looked very grumpy and very fierce!

"Who is that?"

"He is Tricky the Triceratops."

"A Ricerops? What's one of those?" asked Henry in awe.

"No, Henry: Try-seh-ruh-tops."

Henry Owl remembered it now. Triceratops was a herbivore from the same period in time as the *Tyrannosaurus rex*, and they were the deadliest of enemies, each just as capable of killing the other.

"You aren't going to fight him are you?" Henry asked timidly.

"Not if I can help it, Henry - I just want to get home," replied Toothy, "Be a good chap and just pop up to the top of that tree over there."

Henry flapped over to the tall pine tree Toothy had indicated, and watched as the two legends of the Dinosaur world faced off.

"Move aside, Tricky, I'm in a hurry and I don't want to fight with you today!" declared Toothy.

Tricky scuffed his feet in the dusty ground and snorted mockingly, and lowered his head ready to charge.

"Why? Are you afraid your new friend might see you get hurt?" said Tricky, nodding his head in Henry's direction and freeing a big dribble of snot that lazily globbed its way onto the ground with a splat.

"No, Tricky; I just want to get home to my family!" Toothy pleaded.

"Too bad!" roared Tricky, and he charged.

Henry watched as Toothy tensed and crouched, making ready; the muscles in his huge back legs bulged and rippled with power. Toothy's timing was perfect. Just as Tricky was about to impale him with his deadly horns, Toothy hopped to one side and deftly spun around, and slapped Tricky on the bottom with his enormous tail. Smack! It sent Tricky sprawling in the dust - and made him madder still. Henry was amazed at how fast such enormous dinosaurs could move, especially Toothy.

They both squared off again.

"I said I don't want to fight you, Tricky!" Toothy repeated in a menacing growl, as he slowly backed up against the massive pine tree that was sheltering Henry.

"Well, I do! ROAR!" bellowed Tricky as he mounted a fresh assault on Toothy and charged towards them.

Henry was really worried that his friend would get hurt, just as Tricky had threatened, but really he need not have been. Like two immensely powerful and tightly coiled springs, Toothy's hind legs safely catapulted him over Tricky as he sped towards them. Then Henry felt two Earth shattering thumps. One was Toothy landing, which made Henry's tree shake. The second and most powerful was when Tricky hit Henry's tree at full speed. As he smashed into the trunk, his two large horns stabbed deep into it and he was stuck tight! The shock of the impact almost threw Henry from the tree!

Tricky was snarling and roaring lots of rude things and he was shaking the tree so violently that Henry decided the best thing would be to fly back onto Toothy's head.

"Come on Henry, let's go!" commanded Toothy. "He's going to be stuck here for a while."

"Why is he so cross with you?" asked Henry as they resumed their journey once more.

"Tricky? Probably because I ate one of his friends."

Henry was shocked. Not because of the eating thing - he was used to the fact that some dinosaurs ate other dinosaurs - but because of how big a Triceratops was.

"You ate one of those?"

"Well, not all of it,. I had to take it home - but I can't carry something that big in my mouth, and my small fore legs can't really hold much either, they are good for pushing me up after a snooze, but not much more. So I ate as much as I could, and carried the rest back home to share with my

23

family. I think he's still a bit grumpy about it."

Henry could see why Tricky would be a bit upset, so would he if one of his friends had been gobbled up. Henry wanted to know more about his now second favourite Dinosaur, and as they continued on their way to Toothy's nest, he asked some more questions.

"Are they easy to catch Toothy?"

"What?" Toothy had already forgotten Tricky in his haste to get home. Henry continued.

"A Triceratops, they seem very dangerous."

"They are! But if you're careful you should be okay. The best way is to track their scent and sneak up on them up-wind before they know you are there. Most of the time it's easy, but if they spot you, they will charge right at you with those big horns you just saw, and they have very fast reflexes."

"What's a reflex?"

"It means they can think and move very fast," Toothy explained.

"Have you ever been hurt by one?" asked Henry.

"Nearly," replied Toothy. "Twice actually, the second was back there with Tricky, the first was when I was twelve," explained Toothy.

"Have any of your kind been killed by one?"

"Sometimes." said Toothy, he continued. "Now and then I hear of it. It's usually youngsters and the older and slower of us that get caught out."

Toothy slowed, and stopped, peering around.

"Aha, here we are."

Toothy began to make strange soft roaring and grunting sounds.

"What are you doing?" asked Henry.

"I'm calling out to my wife," he explained, "To let her know I'm here and not to attack me."

Henry was curious about this and looked around himself at all the dense jungle foliage. Toothy let out another of his rumbling chuckles.

"Don't worry little friend, you are quite safe now."

The tall wall of trees and branches in front began to rustle and then made the same grunting sounds back. The branches parted as another *Tyrannosaurus rex* poked its head out. Upon seeing Toothy it came all the way out.

The new and smaller Tyrannosaurus looked pleased to see Toothy, but its expression quickly changed to one of concern. Henry guessed this must be Toothy's wife. She was accompanied by a smaller version of herself with feathers on it.

"Oh thank goodness you are back Toothy - something terrible has happened."

She was so fraught she had not seen Henry on top of Toothy's head yet.

"Rani, what's the matter?" asked Toothy, the panic in his wife's eyes clear to see.

"It's the Troodons - they've stolen all our eggs! All five! I just turned my back for a few seconds so I could clean Leela here, and when I turned back, they were gone. What are we to do?"

It sounded very bad to Henry.

"What are Tro-oh-dons, Toothy?" asked Henry.

Rani stepped back. She had just noticed Henry on her husband's head.

"What have you got on your head, Toothy!" she demanded.

"Oh, this is Henry Owl. He's a friend of mine."

"Hello, Henry, I'm Rani - Toothy's wife - and this is our youngest daughter, Leela."

"Hello, Henry," said the youngster. "Are you going to help us find our eggs?" she asked, innocently.

"No, Leela," interrupted Rani, "Of course he's not, how can he help?

He's only a…" she paused and then looked at her husband. "What exactly is he?"

"He's an Owl," explained Toothy.

"Yes Leela, he's only a little Owl."

"No I'm not!" protested Henry, "I'm a Snowy Owl, and I'm eight and three quarters."

"Where is Castellan?" asked Toothy, realising his son's absence.

"He's gone out to search, but so far nothing." explained Rani.

Toothy chewed on his lip in thought. "Hmm, perhaps we should call him back; I'd hate to lose him as well."

Rani nodded, then lifted her head up, extended her neck, tilted her head back and let out a deafening call that sounded like all the elephants and lions in the world, roaring and trumpeting at the same time; her call echoed through the jungle valley. Moments later another roar replied, then presently the sound of stomping grew louder and seemed to be coming from behind as another very heavy pair of feet approached at great speed. In less than sixty heart beats a young Tyrannosaurus crashed into the clearing. At about nine feet tall he was half the height of Toothy. He had similar colours to Rani and Toothy, but unlike Leela, no feathers. Henry decided not to push the question about the Troodons again, he also thought it best not to ask why Leela had feathers, but not Toothy, Rani or Castellan. Maybe later.

"Hey, Dad," puffed Castellan. "Where've you been? What's that on your head?"

"Never mind about that," said Toothy firmly, "We need to sort this disaster out. Did you have any luck tracking them?"

"A bit, but I lost the scent after a while, and the trees are too big for me to push through."

It was at this point that, as he glanced up at the sky, Henry had an idea.

"Hey, everyone, listen," Henry said, with as much authority as he could muster.

They all stopped and looked at him, waiting expectantly.

Chapter 3
The Hunt is On

enry had just seen another small flock of three Pterosaurs circling, riding on a thermal high up. He was ready to bet that they could help. Toothy and his family could not see why the pterosaurs would have anything to do with them, but had to agree with Henry that it was at least worth a try.

As Henry flew higher, he felt a lot lighter. It was not so hot or damp up in the sky, and it was nice to have the sun on his back. As he got nearer, to the pterosaurs, he could hear their raucous calls. Finally, and very out of breath he reached them. They were huge! They had massive wings that were easily seven metres across, long thin heads and beaks with a long pointy bit at the rear ends.

"Hey, guys," he called.

Breaking from their graceful wheeling flight, they took up formation around Henry, curious at the feathery little pipsqueak that had just joined them.

"Hey, Aalia man, what the flappety flap is this?" asked one of the big pterosaurs as he swooped by. Another, presumably Aalia, replied.

"Beats me Eadan, too big to eat whatever it is."

"Hey, don't try to eat me, you're my ancestors!" objected Henry, knowing perfectly well that they weren't but hoping that the pterosaurs were too air-headed to know that.

The flying reptiles all started laughing again.

"Come on, fluff dude, we're only joking with you! We only eat, like, fish man," soothed the third one.

"Yeah, fluff dude, Cahir's right, why don't you kick back with us, uh…" Aalia paused, then continued. "Yeah, like, what are you dude? I like, never saw a saur like you before."

Eadan swooped by again, nearly taking Aalia's head off with his wing.

"Boosh! Yo! Aalia man, you're like, so a poet!" he exclaimed.

Aalia was quick to reply.

"Totally, give me some membrane brah!"

These pterosaurs were funny, Henry had no idea they would be so laid back.

SLAP! Aalia and Eadan slapped their wings together in a complicated daredevil aerial manoeuvre.

"I'm Henry; I'm an owl," chuckled Henry. "I'm not a dinosaur. What kind of dinosaurs are you?"

The Pterosaurs all stopped swirling, and just hovered around Henry.

"Hey, little man!" Cahir addressed . "We're not dinosaurs, dude." He continued.

"Oh, sorry, I thought you all were, even Pterosaurs."

"No biggie!" exclaimed Aalia, "Everyone gets it wrong. We're Pteronodons."

"Yeah," encouraged Eadan, "You know what the big difference is little man?"

Henry wasn't too sure.

"You have wings, they don't?"

"No, man, we get to poop on everyone's heads!" chortled Cahir.

That was it, they all, including Henry, nearly crashed into each other for laughing so much. But Henry was still mindful of his promise to Toothy.

"Listen, guys, I've got a problem." said Henry wiping tears of mirth from his eyes.

The Pteronodons all quietened down.

"So, what up?" asked Eadan.

Henry pointed down to the jungle clearing below, in which everyone could see the Tyrannosaur family.

"You see them down there? That big one is Toothy, he's my friend, but his family have had their eggs stolen by the Troodons, and - well, we need your help to find them."

The Pteronodons were stunned! Aalia was the first to speak.

"Whoah, you're like friends with the carno?"

"The what?" asked Henry.

"The carnosaur – the meat eater, the meat-eating giant lizard – man, you so rock!" Aalia was clearly impressed, as were the others.

"But can you help?" pressed Henry.

Cahir piped up.

"Yeah, man, I saw them, like, take the eggs, while the not-so-little lady down there was washing her kid. They went that way."

He was pointing towards the nearby beach, which Henry would not have seen or heard yet because of the thick jungle. Even so, it wasn't too far away, only a few minutes of running for Toothy and his family.

Henry and the Pteronodons flew out over the beach. A more accurate way of describing it would be as a hot spring beach made out of rocks, where every now and then huge jets of steam shot out of the holes

dotted thereabouts.

There, next to a big hot geyser was a bunch of five small feathery dinosaurs, they looked almost like birds, apparently trying to open the eggs by bashing them on the rocks.

"I've got to get back to Toothy!" exclaimed Henry.

"No time to waste, fluff dude, catch on to my feet!" ordered Aalia.

Henry did as he was instructed, and instantly he was being whooshed back to the clearing.

Chapter Four
Safe Once More

ack at the nest, Toothy was getting worried. He couldn't quite remember what the air-head pterosaurs ate, but he was sure it wasn't anything as big as Henry. It was Castellan who noticed Henry's imminent arrival.

"Look out Dad! In-coming!"

Henry dropped out of the sky like a bolt of lightning and swooped back up to the far side of the clearing.

"This way, Toothy! Follow me, guys, we know where the eggs are! It's this way!"

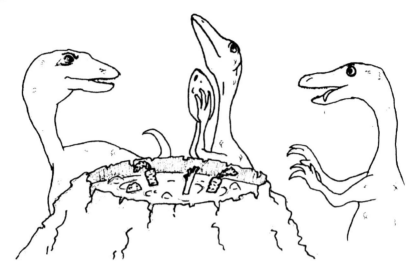

The Tyrannosaurs didn't need telling twice,. With the briefest of glances at each other, they all stomped off in the direction of Henry and the Pteranodons, growling with dreadful menace. It didn't take long to reach the edge of the jungle.

It must have been a terrifying sight for the feathery Troodons on the rocky shore, when the family of Tyrannosaurs exploded from the jungle, sending splinters of tree flying everywhere, bellowing dire threats of slowly being eaten up in earth-shattering roars.

One of the Troodons was frozen in the middle of the act of dropping an egg into a hot pool of water. Henry used the confusion to his advantage and dive-bombed it and landed on its head with a thwump. Henry dropped from the dazed dinosaur, just as it dropped the egg, which landed on Henry's back and knocked him to the ground, pinning him down with its weight – but the egg was safe, and though Henry was winded, he was unharmed.

The Tyrannosaurs sent the Troodons scrambling for their lives and they squeaked and squawked in fear as they scattered, and flapped their way off, finally being chased off by the Pteronodons, who, Henry could hardly dare to bring himself to believe, were actually dive-bombing them and dropping what looked suspiciously like giant bird poops on their heads!

Little Leela bobbed up to Henry.

"You were so brave, Henry Owl," she said as she gently lifted the egg from Henry's back with her mouth.

Rani stomped over, tears of relief and joy in her eyes. She opened her mouth for Leela to gently drop the egg in. Henry could see the other four in there, carefully held down by her tongue.

The Pteronodons landed a short distance away after returning from the chase.

"Man!" exclaimed Cahir. "I feel half a stone lighter already!" They all sniggered in childish delight; their chase certainly had been huge fun.
Toothy lurched over to the Pteronodons.

"Boys, I want to thank you for your help. Without you, our eggs would have been lost. Thank you so much."

"No sweat, dude." replied Eadan.

"Yeah, man it was totally awesome meeting you." expounded Aalia.

"Anyway, we, like, gotta split now! Time for some fishing; later, dudes!"

With that the huge Pterosaurs faced the wind, unfolded their

gigantic membrane-covered wings, which billowed like sails and softly lifted them back up into the air like kites. As they departed, Henry could only make out a few last words from them.

"When I evolve, I wanna be like the fluff dude – he so rocks!"

Henry had no idea who said this, but it did make him feel good inside.

"Henry."

It was Toothy. He continued. "Henry, you were so brave today, as brave as my boy Castellan! If you were my son, I'd be proud to be your dad!"

Toothy looked at Castellan.

"My boy, you have made me the happiest father in the world. Can you go and take your mum and sister back to the nest? I have to take Henry home now."

Henry was suddenly forlorn. He had forgotten all about his family in all the excitement. He had learnt so much!

"But..." he began to protest.

"No, Henry, I'm a dad. I know your parents will be worrying about you. I have to get you through that cave over there, before the magic closes and traps you here forever."

Henry nodded. He knew that his friend was right, even though he didn't like it. They walked back to the cave where they had first met, seventy million years in the future. It wasn't as wet as it was then, it was nice and dry. As they got closer, Henry felt the tingle of magic again; he felt his heart trill with it.

"Will I see you again?" he asked, knowing the real answer deep down.

"Maybe." replied Toothy, smiling. "Maybe."

"I'm going to miss you," said Henry, his little heart beginning to break with sadness, a tear running down his beak.

"I shall miss you too, little owl!"

Henry tried to smile. He didn't mind being called a little owl, really - not by someone as special as Toothy.

And so, Henry, not wanting to take his eyes off his friend, walked backwards into the cave, and left the warmth of the Cretaceous behind. The entrance of the cave shone bright, and Toothy was no more than a silhouette which slowly faded into the brightness, forcing Henry to shut his eyes.

When he opened them again, there he was in the dark wet cave by the seaside. His eyes were beginning to adjust to the darkness. He was just about to take a step back to the entrance which had begun to fizzle into view again, when he spotted something by his feet. The tooth. And just to the left, there was poor old Toothy, just a big old pile of bones again. Henry frantically tried to put the tooth back in, but to no avail.

"Please, come back," he sobbed.

Nothing happened. Then the tooth buzzed in his hands. He was beginning to think it had all been his imagination. Then he heard Toothy in his head.

"Don't be sad, Henry. I've had my time, now it's your turn. Come on, your mummy and daddy will be wondering where you have been."

Henry smiled and walked out of the cave into the hot summer sun. Toothy was right, it was time to go. He looked back at the cave one more time, but it had disappeared. There was no doubt at all. It had all happened!

Henry picked his way back over the rocks and then scuttled as fast as he could back to his own family. They were going to be very worried - he had been gone for hours! Maybe even all day!

He slid to a halt at the beach blanket where his sisters had just settled for a spot of sunbathing. He smirked as they both shrieked at him for kicking sand all over their suntan lotion, but he wasn't scared of them anymore, he'd dive bombed a Troodon!

"I'm so sorry," he blurted. "I didn't mean to be gone for so long, it's just that, the tooth, and..."

Mummy Owl interrupted him, looking very confused.

"What do you mean Henry? Slow down, we've only just got here, I thought you were off looking for Dinosaurs."

Henry smiled. Magic indeed. He looked down at Toothy's big tooth clutched firmly in his wing.

"Oh, yes, you bet I was!" he said knowingly with a big grin on his face.

Henry was now sure of one thing and one thing only. This was going to be the first of many magical adventures this summer holiday!

Henry Owl and the Honey Thief

Chapter One
Poorly and Trapped

enry Owl is an eight year old Snowy Owl, and today he was in bed: bored! Actually, it was worse than that – he was also poorly. If there is one thing worse than being bored, it's being poorly AND bored. Just two weeks into the summer holiday, he'd caught the dreaded owl pox. It just wasn't fair! It was hot and sunny, the paddling pool was out and he was stuck in his stuffy bedroom. It was a good job Daddy Owl had set up a TV and DVD player to help keep him entertained, but even that got a bit tedious in time. He sighed heavily and sat up. He sighed again and looked at his bedside table; his clock said half past ten. Then there was a gentle knock on the door, shortly followed by the appearance of Daddy Owl.

"Hey, how's my poorly boy?" he enquired.

"Bored."

"Look what I've got for you."

Daddy Owl lifted something up he was hiding behind his back. It was Henry's dinosaur tooth. He'd carefully drilled a hole through it and threaded a length of string through to make it into a pendant for Henry.

"My tooth! You've done it! Thanks, Dad."

"No problem, do you want to put it on? It might make you feel better..."

Henry eagerly put it around his neck, clearly waiting for something to happen.

"Well?" enquired Daddy Owl.

Henry shook his head sadly.

"No, nothing, I still feel the same!"

"Perhaps magic teeth don't work on owl pox germs."

Daddy Owl could see that Henry was a little disappointed, and tried his best to cheer him up.

"Would you like me to get a DVD or something? How about Doctor Hoot?"

Henry enjoyed Doctor Hoot's adventures in time and space, but didn't fancy any TV this morning, and shook his head.

"Nah, I'm okay, thanks, I think I'll read one of my comics."

"Well if you're sure."

Daddy Owl leant over Henry and pecked him a gentle kiss on the forehead.

"I'll be up later with some lunch and a drink."

With that, Daddy Owl left Henry to his comic and his new dinosaur tooth pendant.

Henry laid back against his pillows and held his tooth up and gazed at it, holding it so that the sun shone through the hole and

made a small spot of light on Henry's forehead - it was quite large, too big to be a pendant, really. It was curved and sharp at one end, and thick and jagged at the other, with smooth grooves running along the length of it to the tip. He remembered his adventure with Toothy, just as the school summer holiday had started: the fight with Tricky; the search for the eggs; fun skylarking with the air-head Pteronodons and then the fight with the Troodons.

That was nearly three weeks ago and nothing had happened since. In fact, he was beginning to think the tooth's magic had run out.

He placed his tooth back around his neck, slipped out of bed and padded over to the window to see what was going on in the garden. It was just as he'd expected: lovely and sunny.

There was a buzzing and rapid clicking sound nearby; it was a bee trapped in his room flying against the window.

"Oh, you poor thing," he said.

Henry opened the side window so the bee could get out. The

bee stopped and looked quizzically up at him.

"I wonder what you're thinking," he mused to himself.

Henry was so engrossed with the bee that he didn't notice the tooth around his neck begin to buzz.

"It must be awful to feel trapped, I feel trapped because I'm poorly, but you're not poorly."

The bee just buzzed back at him.

"I wish I could understand you," Henry continued.

"Well I can understand you," said the bee in a very highly pitched voice.

Henry Owl blinked in surprise and stepped back.

"Y...you can understand me?"

"Yes, I can."

"And I can understand you, and that must mean..."

Henry looked at his tooth, it was glowing and buzzing! At last! The magic was back.

"Thank you for opening the window to let me out, it's very kind of you. My head was really beginning to hurt."

"That's all right," said Henry. "I wish I could go with you; I'd love to find out about life in your hive."

Henry still hadn't noticed his tooth buzzing, or that his room had begun to grow bigger around him.

"It looks like you are about to get your wish; you're shrinking!" said the bee. "Quick, jump up onto your window ledge, before it's too late."

Realising he was getting smaller, he hopped up next to the bee and within seconds he was the same size.

Chapter Two
Up, Up and Away

W ow!" exclaimed Henry, looking around at his room. "Everything looks so big from here."

"Does it? I suppose if you're not used to it, it might. My name's Belle by the way," the bee replied, glancing at Henry.

"I'm Henry, Henry Owl, pleased to meet you."

Henry held out a wing for Belle to shake, but she just looked at it.

"What's wrong with your wing?" she asked.

"Oh, nothing," said Henry, suddenly feeling silly. "It's just part of how we say hello to each other. We shake wings."

"Right, I see," she said, realisation dawning.

She reached one of her forelegs forward and took Henry's proffered wing and solemnly shook it.

"Now, where we come from," she continued, "this is how we say hello."

She leant forwards and tickled Henry Owl's face all over with her

antennae. It tickled and made him giggle and wriggle – it was definitely a more fun way of saying hello.

"What's it like being a bee?" he asked.

"Busy," she replied, and then she had a thought. "Why don't you climb up onto my back? Come with me and find out."

With one flap of his wings he was landing on the softest fur he had ever felt, she was sumptuously velvety and warm. She had stripes of orange and brown and two pairs of wings on each side. Henry could see that the front wing and hind were held together with tiny hooks, like Velcro. Her wings were like huge panes of shiny glass, with veins running through them. Up this close they shone and sparkled with flashes of red and blue, and it looked like they might have magic in them too.

"Are you ready?" she asked.

Henry nodded.

"Hold on tight!"

And then they were off, up, up and away, out of the window into the gorgeous summer's day.

It wasn't as noisy as Henry had expected, but it was a lot of fun, and the world looked like a very different place. The wind was warm on his face and it made his feathers ruffle.

"Mmm, the air smells lovely," he commented. "What's that sweet smell?"

"That would be the scent of pollen and nectar."

"It's delicious!"

"Yeah? You just wait till we land on that flower down there."

They swooped down towards the grassy ground on which was growing a patch of pale blue wild scabious. When they landed, the aroma was so intense Henry was sure he'd be able to eat the air he was breathing. From Belle's back, Henry watched as she rummaged around in the flower, kicking up big yellow blobs of stuff everywhere.

"Is that yellow snow?" he asked.

"Oh, that's not snow, it's pollen, and it's very important to us bees. It's also important to the plants, but yellow snow is completely different – never eat yellow snow!"

"Why is it important?"

"Well, we use it to feed the baby bees, and the plants need it so they can make seeds that grow into more plants and more flowers for us bees."

Henry hopped down so he could have a look at some pollen. As he landed, it puffed up around him like a cloud and began to stick to him. He watched Belle as she scraped her body all over with her legs, removing it and squashing it onto her hind legs where she had shaped it into large yellow blobs. The next thing that happened took Henry completely by surprise. A long black tube thing dropped down from her head and she began to stick it into the flower.

"What is that?" was Henry's incredulous enquiry.

She pulled it back out and wiggled it about.

"What this? It's my proboscis, it's what I use to reach nectar at the bottom of flowers."

"What's a bobosis?"

"Pro-bos-sis: it works like a straw; it's my tongue."

For a moment Henry thought it a bit weird to have a straw for a tongue, but then he thought , if all you ate was nectar and pollen, you probably didn't need anything else. She then started dribbling on the pollen and squishing more of it onto her legs.

"Why are you spitting on the pollen if you are taking it back to feed the hive?" he asked, feeling a little sick.

"Oh this isn't spit, it's nectar that I've drunk. I'm regurgitating some to stick the pollen together better. It also makes it taste sweeter."

Henry realised what regurgitate meant. If she had just drunk the nectar, and was now bringing it back up...

"Do you want to try some?" she broke a bit off and handed it to him on one of her clawed feet.

"Eugh – that's gross that is! It's worse than I thought, you're sicking up on it – gross! No thanks."

With a "whatever" shrug, Belle placed the lump of pollen back onto her hind leg and then drank some more nectar. She turned to him when she'd filled up.

"Come on Henry, time to go back. Would you like to see the hive?"

Would he ever!

"Oh, yes, please!"

He jumped onto her back again and they took off.

Chapter Three
The Hive

Henry and Belle made it to the hive in no time at all. It was one of five at the bottom of Mr and Mrs Badger's garden.

"How do you know which one is which? They all look the same," he said.

"Oh, that's easy," she replied. "Each hive has its own distinctive smell – mine smells like egg and bacon sandwiches."

Henry thought she was being serious.

"Really?" he said in dubious amazement.

Belle was giggling away.

"No, silly, not really, it's to do with minute things called scent molecules. Each hive has its own mix, and I can smell them with my super sensitive antennae. That and I can remember land marks on the way, and when we get closer you can see that my hive is slightly different from the others. For instance, there is a small patch of moss by the opening on mine: that's also how I can tell."

They began to descend.

"That's my hive there in the middle."

"Do you have anything to do with your neighbours?" he asked.

"No, not really, we might say hello now and then, but that's as far as it goes, we're all too busy in all honesty."

Belle swooped down and landed on the platform that led to the wide narrow opening of the hive; Henry Owl could smell the rich sweet scent of honey as it wafted out of the hive. Belle walked towards the opening.

"Hold it right there you two!" an assertive deep female voice bellowed.

Belle froze in her tracks. For a moment, she had forgotten about Henry not being a bee.

"Turn around and identify yourselves!"

Belle obeyed, as she turned Henry caught sight of the bossy bee. It was very hard to tell the difference between the two bees, especially with literally hundreds of other bees buzzing here and there all around them. In fact, it was very confusing for Henry.

"Belle, bee number 59212."

"And who is that you are carrying with you?"

"This is Henry, he's a friend."

The other bee walked right up to them and began sniffing Henry with her feelers.

"What exactly is it?" the bossy guard bee asked in a mixture of curiosity and disgust.

"Hey!" Henry exploded in defiance. "*It* is not an *it*, and *it* has a name!" he finished testily.

The guard bee stepped back in mock surprise.

"Whoa there little June bug, I was only asking."

"And I'm not a June bug, I'm an Owl, Henry Owl and I'm eight years old!"

Belle intervened.

"Listen, Rosemary," (this was the name of the guard bee). "I know we're not supposed to bring other people into the hive, but I owe Henry – he saved my life; he let me out of his room. If it weren't for him, I'd never have made it back."

Rosemary looked pointedly at Henry. Belle could almost read her mind so she continued to persuade the guard.

"I know he's small, but he wasn't before. Some kind of magic made him like this – it's like he has been rewarded for his kindness to me."

Rosemary paused a moment in thought.

"Magic? If you say so! Just for today then, okay?"

"Just today," Belle agreed. "Can I get on? I have pollen and nectar to drop off."

Rosemary snorted, and nodded, and then she was off to bother someone else. When she was safely out of ear-shot Henry ventured a question.

"What's her problem?"

"Rosemary?" Belle replied. "Don't worry about her, she's just a bossy boots – all brawn and no brain."

"What's brawn?" Henry asked.

"You know, a muscle head, a bully."

"Oh." Henry murmured, not really understanding what she meant.

"Anyway," she continued, as they went in, "everyone's on high alert right now. Apparently, honey has been going missing in the middle of the night."

Who would be daft enough to steal honey from a hive of bees? Henry thought to himself.

"Missing? How?" he asked.

"There's a honey thief, Henry, and no one knows who it is."

The sweet warm darkness of the hive swallowed them. Thanks to Henry's owl eyes, specially evolved, he was able to see clearly in the dark. He could see thousands of bees bustling everywhere, and the buzzing hum was very loud indeed.

"How can you think in all this racket?" he asked, stuffing some feathers into his ear holes, to block out some of the noise.

"You just get used to it. Look up there."

Henry looked up. Stretching all the way up into the darkness, where even his eyes couldn't see, were huge rows of honey combs, thousands of perfect hexagons – all smothered in bees. Wide-eyed, he gasped.

"WOW!" was all he could think of to say. He wondered out loud how many bees lived in the hive.

"There's about eighty thousand of us, one of whom is the Queen, my mother, and sometimes I might have a bunch of brothers."

Sometimes brothers? That was a strange thing to say.

"What do you mean sometimes you have brothers?"

Henry thought Belle might begin to get tired of all his questions, but she seemed quite happy to answer them.

"Well," she began, "sometimes, like now, the hive gets too big and a new Queen and some drones are made . The drones are male bees – so they're my brothers."

Henry only had older sisters.

"What are they like, the drones?"

"Hah," she snorted. "Big and lazy, all they do is lounge about, laughing and joking, and stuff their faces with honey, pollen and nectar."

"Why doesn't anyone do anything about it?" he asked.

"No point really. They get kicked out for the mating flight, so we get rid of them in the end because they are too dense to find their way back; any that are left in the autumn are either driven out or killed."

Belle watched Henry looking at the hive and all her sisters - always in constant motion. She could see he was about to ask about the mating so decided to answer the question before he asked.

"The mating happens when we have a new Queen, like I said, one of which we have at the moment. She flies out when she is ready, and we kick the drones out after her, they chase after her and mate on the wing. Then the new Queen comes back and then we decide what to do with the hive."

"What do you do with the hive?"

"Most of the time, the old Queen leaves with a group of workers to start a new hive, but sometimes she doesn't want to, and that's where the trouble begins."

Henry thought that sounded serious.

"What do you mean trouble?"

"Well, if the old Queen doesn't want to leave, then they fight over who gets to rule the hive – often it's to the death, and usually it's the old Queen who is killed."

Henry was aghast!

"But that's terrible!"

"Why?" was Belle's confused response.

"Because the old Queen's daughter kills her, that's why; it's like me killing my mum!"

"But it's always been this way," Belle patiently explained. "It's how the hive is kept strong, especially if the old Queen is really *old*, like two to three seasons old."

Henry paused.

"Do you think I could get to meet the Queen?"

"No, she'll be too busy laying eggs, but I expect I could introduce you to the new Queen, we might bump into her as I'm showing you around."

Belle stopped walking.

"Right, this is where it starts, the nursery."

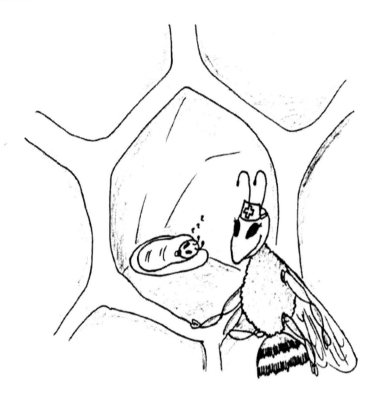

Henry looked all around himself; the constant flow of bees was endless. He looked into some of the hexagonal honeycombs. He could see a tiny little white speck in each one.

"What are these?" he asked.

"Oh," said Belle, surprised. "These are eggs, newly laid too by the looks of things, which means the old Queen might be nearby, so you could be in luck after all."

Henry could see some bees poking their heads into the cell in the combs.

"What are they doing?"

"They are nurse bees; they are looking after the eggs and grubs.

They lick the eggs and grubs to keep them clean and feed the growing grubs with pollen, honey, a bit of saliva and nectar – we call it bee bread. They also get rid of the waste..." Belle trailed off.

"Waste?" Henry interjected.

"Yes, waste, poo, if you like. It's the first job a bee gets in the hive."

Belle took Henry to some nearby cells to show him some larger grubs. He saw funny-looking maggot-like things squirming around in each cell.

"In this one, you can see a grub that is about to pupate."

"Eugh!"

"No Henry, pupate, not poop, it means to make a cocoon and turn into a bee, like me."

"Oh!" exclaimed Henry. "So you were a maggot..."

"Grub." Corrected Belle.

"Grub like this once."

"Yes," she said, pleased that her student was getting it.

Henry, noticed some of the cells had thick dome-shaped caps on them.

"What's wrong with these ones?"

Belle sniffed one with her feelers.

"Nothing at all, these are the ones that are pupating. In a few days' time, some of these will emerge as a bee, just like me. They grow so fast, three days as an egg, six days from hatchling to pupa, then ten days later out comes the new bee."

It was amazing in the hive, it made Henry Owl feel quite dizzy. He looked around to see if anyone wasn't doing anything – he found no one; there wasn't a single bee, apart from Belle, standing idle.

"It looks as though everyone has something to do." He observed.

"That's right, a few days after a bee emerges, it is straight to work and doesn't stop until it dies, except, maybe at night, where we all come back to the hive to roost and rest."

Henry just couldn't stop thinking; his head was just too full of questions and the desire to learn everything he could about the life of a bee.

"What jobs do you do?"

"Hmm." Belle thought for a moment. "That depends, really, because we have different jobs at different times and ages - sometimes, we can go from one job to another, and then back again, but mostly it goes like this. First, we make the wax for the builder bees, who build new combs or repair damaged parts. Then, we might move on to nursery duties, or building, or alternatively we might be nursery bees first of all, before the wax and building. Then, we move outside as foragers or scout bees – my current job - going out to find the best places, then come back to tell everyone about it."

"How can you tell everyone? There's thousands of you, and how can you be heard over this noise?"

"A brilliant question, Henry, but one that is easily answered. Watch this."

Belle suddenly began to dance, circling to the left, waggling her abdomen, circling right, waggling again, and then kept repeating it. Some of the passing bees noticed and ambled over to them. They began touching Belle with their antennae - and got excited. They then began copying Belle's dance, then more bees near them took it up until there was an enormous bee-dance frenzy.

"What's going on?" asked Henry.

"I've told them all where the best flowers are to be found! Now they are passing the message around and very soon thousands of foragers are going to follow the directions I gave and arrive in your garden to harvest pollen and nectar from your Mum's flower borders."

It was hard to believe that that one simple dance could give all of that information, but Henry saw no reason for Belle to be playing tricks on him, so it must be true.

"Come on," Belle prompted. "Let's go see the builders at work."

Chapter Four
The Hornets Attack

 hortly, they reached an area of the hive where the wax turned from yellow to creamy white.

"What's wrong with this part of the hive?" asked Henry.

"Nothing, it's new - look," said Belle. "Some of the comb is still to be completed." Henry looked and saw that some of the wax cells were half finished. Something white fell from above and boinked him on the head.

"Ow! What was that?" he demanded.

It landed on the floor next to him. It was a large flat splat-shaped thing. Belle looked at it casually.

"Oh, that's a bit of new wax; it's fallen from one of our young bees. I'd keep an eye out above if I were you, there's plenty more where that came from."

No sooner had Belle finished her sentence, han another bee scampered past, grabbed it and took it away to be used for building more honey comb. Henry looked up. At the top of the hive was an enormous mass of bees hanging from each other, all of them stretching themselves rather thin; they looked like an enormous bee curtain.

"Ooh, that looks painful," he mused to himself.

Without thinking, Belle answered him.

"No, not really, all that stretching stimulates their wax making cells, then it just oozes out and falls to the floor, like just now, where builder bees take it away for construction. Basically, the entire hive is made of wax - "

"- and it is all made by yourselves," finished Henry.

Suddenly, Belle went silent, she was motionless, only her antennae were waving around. Moreover, every bee in sight was doing the same.

"Belle?" he nudged her.

Like a wave and without warning, all the bees surged in one direction, Belle snapped out of her trance.

"Henry! Quick! Jump on my back!"

"What's wrong?" he asked as he climbed, an urgent tone in his voice.

"The hive is being attacked, and we all have to defend it."

"But how can I defend the hive? I don't have a sting," he said on the run.

Realising he was right, Belle took him higher up, where he would be safe.

"Stay here!" she instructed, then disappeared into a sea of bees. It was very tempting to go and have a look at what was going on, but on this occasion he thought better of it. How would he be able to find her? All the bees looked identical, and without a pair of super sensitive antennae to sniff her out, he'd never find her, so staying put was the best thing to do. Especially as she came back a few moments later.

"There you are, Henry. This is very important. We are being raided by a pack of hornets, they are very dangerous."

Henry knew about hornets. They were like wasps, but much bigger. He'd seen them once or twice in the woods, but now he was so small, he knew they could easily make a meal out of him.

"It's okay," soothed Belle. "We know exactly what we are doing. Come and see."

She led Henry to the entrance where he could see an ocean of bees facing five enormous hornets. They dwarfed the bees! They looked very menacing.

"Give us your honey and your grubs!" one of the monstrous hornets demanded.

"Or we'll tear you all apart!" another threatened, snapping its fearsome jagged mandibles together with a snap.

"There's something different about these hornets." Henry remarked to Belle. "They aren't like any I've seen before."

"That's because they aren't," she confirmed. "They are Japanese Hornets. They were accidentally introduced into Europe, and sometimes they can get blown across the channel to England. They are bad news – they are hive killers! If just one of those scouts gets back to her nest, this hive, and our neighbours' too, are done for."

"So what are we going to do about it?" he asked desperately.

"We've already started."

"What?"

As far as Henry could see, no one was doing anything.

"What do you mean? No one's moving!"

"Oh yes we are, we've been doing it for the last five minutes or so, ever since the sentry bees saw them approach." She paused dramatically, knowing she had Henry's full attention. "Can you hear the humming noise getting louder?"

Yes, now she mentioned it, there was a definite increase in the level of the sound. Where once it was just a background hum, it was a definite angry buzz.

"What's going on, is everyone going to attack?"

"Oh no, that would be suicide; we are making the hive hotter.

We are vibrating our bodies to generate heat and in a moment hundreds of bees are going to swamp those scouts. Lots will die, but so will the scouts."

"But these hornets are three times as big as you, and one sting will kill you, and hornets and wasps can sting lots of times over..."

Henry was worried for his friend.

"But we won't all be fighting. I can't, because I have to keep an eye on you, but fighting isn't the idea. Cooking them is what we are about to do."

Belle barely had time to finish what she was saying before one brave bee launched herself at a hornet. Henry didn't see what happened to her, because she was instantly followed by a pulsing wave of bees that engulfed the hapless hornets. Yet the bees weren't actually attacking, they were just buzzing in fury. The noise grew and grew until Henry had to shout to be heard.

"Why are you all doing this?"

"Like I said, Henry, we're cooking them. They might be big, have deadly jaws and stings, but we have one trick they don't."

"What's that?" Henry shouted back. He was finding out surprise after surprise in the world of the bee.

"We can make our bodies hot by buzzing them - it generates friction energy. We can survive the heat , mostly, but they definitely can't. Deep inside that mass, it is so hot that even some of my sisters will die."

How could she be so cold?

"Doesn't that make you feel sad?" he asked. "I mean, my sisters are annoying, but I still love them."

"Not really, after all, what are we for if not to defend our hive? We are all the same. The Queen rules, and we obey."

The hum had started to drop, and the pile of bees slowly dispersed. Gradually, a scene of carnage was revealed. Five huge dead hornets were surrounded by fifty or so dead bees. Henry was wondering what had become of the first brave little bee, when a gigantic bee strode forwards to inspect the arena of battle. It was the Queen. Big as she was, she was still dwarfed by the hornets.

"Clear this mess up!" she commanded. "Double the guards, there might be more of them nearby."

Every bee within earshot sprang into action and without a care, they began pushing their fallen sisters out of the hive, where they just dropped them off the edge of the landing platform.

He tried not to let Belle see that this was upsetting him; it didn't work.

"Don't worry, we have thousands of bees in this colony, we can afford to lose a few here and there; none of us are indispensable – even me," she continued. "Come on, let's see if we can find the new Queen."

They were just about to give up looking, when, as they were passing yet another nursery section of the hive, a stern voice from behind called them to a halt.

"Stop right there, you two!"

It was the Queen - the *old Queen.* They slowly turned back around.

"Identify yourselves!" she demanded.

"I am Belle, Your Majesty."

"And I am Henry Owl."

"He's a friend," Belle quickly added.

The Queen appeared to think about this for a second, and then dismissed the irrelevant information from her mind.

"Never mind. Belle, I want you to join my swarm. We will be leaving tomorrow. It would have been today were it not for the hornet scouts."

"As you command, my Queen."

The Queen then turned her compound eyes to Henry.

"So, little owl, what do you do?"

For a moment there, Henry was about to correct her, but quickly thought better of it.

"Me? Um, I can fly and catch mice."

The Queen laughed at him.

"You catch mice? More likely they'd be catching you, I say."

This made Henry feel a little bit embarrassed.

"I'm not normally this small," he mumbled.

"What? What was that?" demanded the Queen. "Speak up, boy, look people in the eye when you talk to them."

"I said I'm not normally this small."

The Queen fixed him with a freezing glance, then he remembered.

"Your Majesty."

The Queen nodded.

"Well, I have no need for a mouse catcher, so you'll have to stay here." She turned back to Belle. "Sunrise on the landing platform." Then she made to leave. Henry remembered the issue about the disappearing honey. As the Queen was walking away, he burst out:

"Your Majesty, has anyone solved the mystery of the honey thief? Was it the hornets after all?"

She froze and turned back to face them.

"You're quite a bold little one, aren't you?" she stated. "No, we haven't solved the mystery, and no, the honey thief is not a hornet. They only attack in the day. The honey thief strikes in the dead of night, when all but a few of us are asleep. Come with me and I'll show you."

She led them back to an area of the hive where the bees were rebuilding. When the bees noticed the approaching party and its leader, they suddenly broke into increased vigour. The Queen pointed a foreleg to an area of comb near the entrance.

"Look at the cells over there, what do you notice?"

Henry looked at the combs, they had a hole in each one.

The Queen continued.

"Hornets don't do that, they just rip the comb open. This is something else, something much bigger and much stronger."

A large slab of wax suddenly plopped down beside Henry. It started an idea growing in his head.

"Does the thief come every night?" he asked.

"Yes," replied Belle.

"Does it always come in the same way?"

"Yes, it does," answered the Queen.

Henry took in all of the waxworks going on. He was smiling; he had a fantastic plan to trap the honey thief bubbling away in his mind.

"Well, out with it boy!" demanded the Queen.

"We could build a trap."

The Queen and Belle looked at each other agog! It was so simple and obvious – why hadn't anyone else thought of this before? All they'd done as a colony was to keep on repairing and refilling the empty combs. Henry was harbouring a suspicion that the mystery raider was nothing other than a mouse, a small, but brave one none-the-less. Perhaps the Queen would need a mouse catcher after all.

"Your Majesty," Henry began. "If we could get the builders to make a big thick wall of wax at the entrance to the hive, one that seals it up, but leave a hole big enough for a mouse to get in, your foragers would still be able to do their work. This means there is only one way in or out, but the wall needs to be very thick mind, which means it will need a lot of wax."

The Queen grunted.

"Well, we have no shortage of that around here."

"Good! Then, we connect a tunnel to the entrance, one that gets narrower at the end, but the tube needs to be very thick too, and at the end we need some bait, a big blob of honey should do the trick."

"We have plenty of that too!" interrupted the Queen, needlessly stating the obvious.

"Brilliant!" Henry said. "Here's what it should look like."

With a clawed toe outstretched he scratched his design into the floor of the hive for Belle and the Queen to see. The old Queen nodded her approval.

"It seems, my boy, I was too hasty in my appraisal of you. A flying mouse catcher is of no use to me, but a clever little owl who can catch a honey thief is worth all the honey, nectar and pollen in this hive! I hope you will consider swarming with us – if of course your plan works."

He had seen some pictures of swarming bees in his nature books at home: they looked fearsome and dangerous! The prospect of being near one, let alone in one, had never entered his imagination.

"Then we'd better get started, your Majesty," he said.

"Very well, I will summon some workers and the wax makers."

She began turning her body around and buzzing her wings. As she completed each turn a sweet smell was wafted over Henry. He couldn't help but breathe it in deeply. It made him feel giddy and for a moment all he could think about was being with the Queen.

"Ooh what's that lovely smell?" he asked in a dreamy voice.

Belle giggled at him. The Queen explained.

"That Henry, is how I control the whole hive. I use something called pheromones."

"Femoonones? What are femoonones?"

"Pheromones, Henry," the Queen irritably explained. "feh-roh-moans – they are special chemicals I make in my body. The one you just experienced is a short-range one, one that is strong enough to control the nearby bees."

Sure enough, moments later they were surrounded by one hundred or so bees.

"My daughters," announced the Queen, "this is Henry Owl. I want you all to listen to him very carefully. He believes he has a very cunning plan to trap the mystery honey thief." Turning to Belle and Henry, she finished off. "You two are in charge here. Belle, I want you to report back to me when the work is finished; I want to inspect it before night falls."

"Yes, my Queen." Belle said.

"I must go and find my successor to bring her up-to-date with these proceedings."

And then she was gone, leaving Henry and Belle with an enormous crowd of eager-looking bees.

"Um," began Henry. He was very nervous. Soon, he found his confidence, and began to relay his plan to his audience. It was beginning to get dark outside, but the wax workers were already dropping a hail storm of pellets, and the wall was already beginning to take shape.

Just as the first of the evening stars came out to listen to the first of the evening cricket songs, the trap was done and the bait set. Belle had long gone to fetch the Queens, who were now both appraising the rather impressive construction.

"Well, mother, it will be interesting to see if this works," said the young Queen.

"Indeed my dear, indeed!"

The workers looked exhausted and the young Queen dismissed them to get rest and called for some replacements – just in case.

"And so we wait!" pointed out the young Queen, quite unnecessarily, trying to sound as important and impressive as her mother.

And wait they did, for quite some time, until suddenly there was a very loud buzzing sound from outside. Everyone immediately thought it to be hornets and drew back a couple of paces, more so when a huge winged shadow fell across the wax wall from outside, but the buzz was too loud and too low in tone to be a hornet. It landed with a big BUMP and settled. Henry was holding his breath. He wondered if bees did the same, but saw that they didn't. They all waited tensely as the huge monster scratched and scraped its way around outside, obviously looking for a way in. Then it spoke.

"Now what have these silly bees been up to? Build a barrier and then forget to finish it off."

"This is it!" whispered Belle.

Henry nodded, hoping his plan was going to work – nobody dared move! The monster began to speak again.

"Oh ho! What do we have here? Hmm, a hole, just big enough for me to fit through! Isn't that convenient! I don't think anyone would think it's a trap!"

Oh no! Henry realised his plan was failing; he saw the two Queens looking furious. The monster carried on talking.

"Ah, silly me, but the wall is too thick for my claws, but what about my proboscis?"

Something sharp and pointed stabbed through the wax barrier near to where Henry was crouching.

"Nope, not too thick at all for me!"

It stabbed through again, this time pulling a large chunk away to reveal an enormous compound eye. The bees all started to buzz nervously. Henry shifted his feet and knocked something over, a stray wax pellet, there were thousands of them lying around, then he had another brilliant idea.

"Quick, everyone!" he hissed. "Grab some wax, now!"

Everyone looked at him, but they didn't move.

"Come on, think! What did you do with the hornets?"

No one answered.

"You swarmed them, so now all you have to do is the same, but with the wax, you all buzz to warm up the wax to soften it, and as the monster breaks through you, swarm it and cover it in the wax to imprison it!"

The old Queen saw how his plan would work.

"He's right, we are many, this monster is but one, all of you, grab as much wax as you can carry, now!"

All the bees flew into action, and just in time too as the monster broke through the wall.

"Aha!" it declared. "I have you now!"

But it was an empty threat, huge though this monster was, it was instantly drowned by hundreds of bees as they fearlessly launched themselves onto the new threat, pinning it down and completely covering it in wax.

"Enough!" bellowed the young Queen, clearly able to see that the creature had been contained; it looked like a battered sausage that was two days old. The bees had done their job well; it was covered from head to toe in wax and couldn't move at all. All that could be heard from it were muffled sounds as it tried to free itself. The old Queen walked up to it and ripped an area of wax away from where she thought the head would be found. It revealed a large fuzzy bulbous head with two compound eyes and a huge dagger-like proboscis. On top of the head were what looked like feelers or antennae. Henry was sure he'd seen something like this in one of his books.

"What and who are you!" The old Queen demanded. "Why are you raiding my hive?"

The creature just glared sullenly back at her.

"Very well," continued the Queen. "It's like that, then, is it?"

She swung her abdomen around and brought the tip of it up close to the creature's eye. Slowly, and with deliberate menace, the Queen poked out her sting, allowing a bead of venom to grow at the tip.

"Did you know," she said in a steady and threatening tone, "that every one of my bees can only sting once, but that one sting will kill them too?" She waited for a response, but one was not forthcoming. "My royal daughter and I on the other hand, can sting as many times as we like, and our stings are very painful – probably deadly to you."

That was enough to break the intruder's resolve.

"All right, I give up! I'm a Death's Head hawk moth, and I need to raid your honey because my proboscis is too short to reach all the nectar in flowers."

All the bees began buzzing in anger.

"Please don't hurt me," pleaded the moth. "I didn't mean no harm."

The Queen wasn't about to let the moth off the hook.

"Explain to us how you have been able to keep stealing honey from us!" She pushed her sting a little closer for emphasis.

The moth revealed its secrets.

"It's not really that difficult once I get past your guards. Some of them attack me, but their stings aren't strong enough to get through my exoskeleton. But I'm not so sure about yours though, it looks very dangerous."

"I dare say it is," replied the Queen. "Shall we put it to the test?"

"No, no, not necessary. Then when I have got past the guards, I start to copy the sounds you make."

This was very interesting. The Queen was wondering what sounds she made the moth could possibly ever hope to copy.

"Such as?" she demanded.

"This."

Then the moth began to make a series of squeaks of varying pitch and loudness. All the gathered bees stepped back and gasped. Whispers echoed around the vicinity of the hive.

"It talks the language of the Queens."

"Silence!" ordered the Queen. "So, you can copy me, but that surely can't be enough to keep you from harm!"

"No it isn't. I also copy the smell you make as well, but when I have drunk your honey, I can no longer squeak, and my smell, which is a bit like how your worker bees smell, is not exactly like yours, because every hive has its own smell, so I have to get out fast before you notice I've been here."

"And how is your plan working?"

The moth looked from the Queen down to the floor of the hive.

"Not very well," it replied sullenly.

From somewhere at the back, an angry bee yelled, "Execute it, your Majesty!"

The Queen had to think long and hard about this. She had to admit, she was very tempted to execute the honey thief. The rest of the bees buzzed in agreement. Then, Henry boldly stepped forward. He cleared his throat.

"Ahem, pardon me, your Majesty, but how about we make an example of it? We can tell the other bees from next door of the tricks these moths play and how to stop them getting away with it. We can keep this one prisoner for now until the other hives have come to see it."

The Queen shook her head.

"A good idea, Henry, but we really are too busy to have anything to do with the hives next door; if they have problems with honey thieves, it's down to them to sort them out. We will just roll it out of the hive and leave it there, maybe a passing bird will see it and eat it."

The Queen turned back to the moth.

"If you survive this, and if you so much as come anywhere near to my hive again, next time you won't be so fortunate! Do you understand?"

The moth nodded.

"To the ledge with it!" the Queen commanded.

All the bees and Henry too assisted in pulling down the wax wall, and then the invader was rolled away, and simply dumped over the edge, squeaking as it disappeared from view. Henry yawned deeply, he felt very tired. Then he noticed that a new day was dawning. He'd not had a wink of sleep. He wasn't the only one to have noticed.

"It's sunrise!" the Queen stated. Her eyes fell on Belle. "Belle, you are a scout bee, find some place away from the hive where it will be safe for us to roost a swarm."

"I already know of such a place my Queen."

The Queen raised an antennae, inviting Belle to continue. Belle took the cue.

"There is a big tree not very far from here, where a very special friend of mine lives."

Henry was beaming, of course, his home tree!

"Yes, your Majesty," he exclaimed. "The home tree! It's perfect! At the top is a big hollow. I used to play in there when I was smaller; it would be ideal for you to make a new hive!"

By now, thousands of bees were massing around them, these were the swarm bees that had chosen to leave with the old Queen. They parted as the younger Queen emerged. The old Queen went over to her daughter.

"Daughter of mine, I surrender the hive to you, rule your sisters well and may you grow many daughters of your own."

"I will, mother of mine. Go in peace, never to return."

Henry was listening.

"What's all that about?" he asked Belle.

"Oh, that's just the leaving ceremony."

Henry grimaced.

"It sounds a bit..." he was trying to think of the right adjective. Belle thought of one for him.

"Cheesy?"

"Yeah, that's it, cheesy."

"Come on, Henry, everyone's looking at us. I think they want you to lead the swarm."

Belle was right, thousands of pairs of compound eyes were looking directly at him, including both of the Queens. Belle dipped her front for

Henry to hop onto her again. And they were off once again, up into the morning air, instantly followed by the thousands of bees that were making up the swarm. The Queen was directly behind them, who in turn was being closely followed by a dense cloud of bees. Henry was in a swarm of bees and he was loving it! He and Belle led the swarm to the home tree where he lived with his family. They flew up towards the top of the tree, and the big hole grew into view. They led the swarm inside. It was cavernous, bigger even than the inside of the old hive. The Queen was very pleased.

"Henry and Belle, you have both served the hive very well. You will always be welcome here amongst us Henry."

"Thank you," he hesitated. "My Queen."

The Queen and Belle laughed. The Queen continued.

"Henry, I think it's time we took you home."

Henry took a last look at the new hive. There was already a curtain of bees hanging from the top of the hollow, and pellets of wax were already raining down and being collected by the workers. It really was true, in his nature books he'd often read about how there is never a quiet moment in honey bee hive life, there was always work to *be* done, and the works was always *being* done.

Reluctantly, Henry climbed back up onto Belle, and she and the Queen flew him back down the tree to where he lived with his family. Henry's bedroom window was wide open, and they flew in. The two bees looked around at how big it was.

"Imagine the hive we could build in here, your Majesty!" exclaimed Belle.

"Hey, this is my room!" objected Henry before he realised Belle was teasing him.

"Thank you for your help, Henry," said the Queen. "In return, I would like to offer you as much honey as you and your family will ever need."

Henry thought about this. His family had never tasted honey, it wasn't on the snowy owl menu. It was something he was going to sort out as soon as he had the chance. He let out another gargantuan yawn, and looked longingly at his bed. The pile of pillows he'd left there yesterday, under his quilt still looked un-disturbed.

"Thank you Belle," he said. "And thank you, your Majesty, I have learned so much about how amazing you bees are, but I'm so sorry; I'm ever so tired - and if I don't get into my bed soon, I'm going to fall asleep where I stand!"

The bees understood, and with a fond tickling of his face with their antennae, they buzzed away out of his window. He looked up at his bed. He'd just remembered he was still the size of a bee.

Feeling exhausted and like he was made of heavy stone, he was preparing to make the flight up to his pillows when his magic tooth began to buzz. He was growing larger again. In moments he was back to his normal size and just about to climb into his soft sheets when his bedroom door opened to reveal Daddy Owl.

"Ah, you're up, are you feeling better? Guess what? We've been invited to Auntie Screech's' baobab tree. How do you fancy a trip to Africa?"

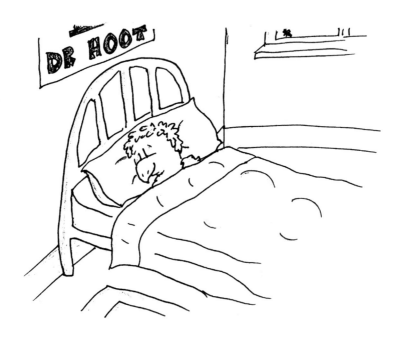

Henry groaned and flopped down onto his bed, asleep and snoring deeply before his head had even hit the pillow.

Henry Owl and the Ivory Hunters

Chapter One
Stampede

frica is hot! In some places, it is not just hot, it is sticky and hot, like in the big rainforests. However, most places are just dry and hot. Like where Auntie Screech lived, in a dead, hollowed out tree, not far from the jungle. His sisters were in their element, all they had done for the last two days was sun bathe. Mummy Owl did not like the heat, and she chose to come out at night time with Daddy and Auntie Screech for the hunts – there were rich pickings to be had out here. Henry, however, liked the day - in fact, he loved it! He crawled his way out of the entrance hole and sat on a branch, breathing in the thick sounds of early morning African life.

It was the middle of the dry season, and the long grasses of the plains were baked crisp and dry, and when the wind blew through them it made it sound like the ground was whispering its secrets to anything that cared to listen. Henry felt a sudden chill and fluffed his feathers up. Even in the plains, the mornings can be cold. Henry already knew it would not last long; with the sun already up, he knew the temperatures were about to rocket.

The insect life here was brilliant, Henry had already met a fearsome Baboon Spider, lots of friendly locusts, who were constantly hungry and some rather snappy scorpions. Suddenly the tree shook. Startled, he searched for the source of the disturbance. The tree continued

to shake and wobble, then he heard a contented sigh.

"Ah, that hits the spot."

Henry hunted out the source of the sounds and found a huge grey-brown monster thing, rubbing its flank against the rough trunk of the tree. It had crinkled skin that looked like bark, a big head, big ears and a long snakey thing hanging from its face with huge curved upwards teeth, or perhaps they were upside down fangs; he'd never seen anything like this before. The creature caught sight of him and stopped its scratching, and spoke in a husky female voice.

"Well, hello there little owl, how are you this fine morning?"

Henry squeaked and hid on the other side of the tree.

"Come on out, little friend, I will not hurt you," coaxed the creature.

"Wh, wh, what do you eat?" Henry asked, still a little nervous.

"Why, I only eat grasses, leaves and vegetation."

Henry poked his head around the tree to have another look at this mysterious creature. He looked warily at the giant fangs.

"You're not another dinosaur are you? I had a magic adventure with a dinosaur once..." his voice trailed off as he remembered his friends from long long ago.

"No, of course I am not, I am an elephant, my name is Kefilwe, it means given."

"What are any pants?" Henry asked, repeating the word completely wrong.

"No, e-leh-fant, it has a silent p and an h to make a fff sound."

"Words are confusing!" Henry said in frustration.

"Yes, they can be. Elephants are gentle animals, we live in herds – that means large groups. We are not dangerous, unless we think our children are in danger, and then we can be nasty, and we also never forget! Are you going to introduce yourself? You know who I am."

Henry was forgetting himself.

"Oh, yes, I'm Henry, Henry Owl, I'm a snowy owl and I'm eight."

Kefilwe was surprised by this and a confused expression appeared on her face.

"But I thought that owls only came out at night."
It was Henry's turn to explain.

"Well, mostly yes, but not with me, I like to be up in the day

95

sometimes, there's just so much to see and do, and if I sleep all through the day I'm going to miss it all. Anyway, we're on holiday so I'm allowed up late, but I have to be in bed when the sun starts to come up when I'm back to school."

For such a little owl, Henry could certainly talk!

"So when do you sleep?" Kefilwe asked.

"When I'm tired," he replied, in a typical eight-year-old fashion.

The friendly elephant moved closer to Henry for a more detailed inspection. She *"Hmmmd."* to herself. She took a step back.

"You are not from around these parts are you?"

"No." he said. "I'm from England."

Kefilwe nodded, "I have heard of it, what is it like there?"

"Wet mostly," he began. "Well, sometimes it's nice, like in the summer when it is sunny, but even then it rains a lot. Sometimes though, it's cold and icy."

The elephant made a 'HARRUMPHING' sound.

"Well here, it is mostly hot and dry. Sometimes we have rain, but only for a little while, sometimes it doesn't rain for more than a year."

No rain for a year! Henry found that hard to imagine.

"But if there's no water, what is there to drink?"

Kefilwe explained further.

"Ah, yes, when it rains, it rains a lot – ever such a lot, and it makes giant lakes and rivers, but when the wet season is gone, it goes very quickly. The lakes and rivers quickly dry up to leave water holes, and then they will evaporate into dust."

"What happens when all the water has emaporated?"

"Ee-vah-pour-ate, Henry, evaporate, it is not very nice!"

Kefilwe swatted at some flies that were buzzing around her head with her trunk; they had gathered at the damp corners of her eyes. She had amazingly long lashes and dark brown eyes.

"Do you like it here, Henry?" she asked. It was a silly question, really.

"Oh, yes, it's fantastic! I just wish I had more time to look around; we go home in two days."

"That is not long at all, how would you like to come see the place with me?"

It was a very tempting offer, but then he remembered his parents' warnings about the dangers of going off with people he didn't know. He hesitated.

"I think I'll go and ask my mum and dad first."

Initially, Mummy Owl wasn't too keen, and she wasn't especially happy about being woken up so early. Auntie Screech, however, was able to sort things out. She explained that she knew Kefilwe, and that Henry would be quite safe with her.

So that was that. He hopped onto her head and they lumbered off for a safari walkabout. Kefilwe was a brilliant guide; she was very wise and knew all of the animals. She showed Henry the lazy lions, ruled over by Kgosi, the nervous zebras, and the graceful gazelles. Finally he met Sethunya, a cheetah mother and her cubs. He was half-way through being introduced to the cheetah cubs when a sharp and explosive CRACK,

echoed and smashed its way across the land. All animals crouched low to the ground, with their ears close against their heads.

"What was that?" whispered Henry. "It can't be far away."

"That is a gun Henry!" said Kefilwe. "We need to get away from here now, there are hunters nearby."

"Shouldn't we get back to my auntie's tree?" protested Henry.

"No! It's too dangerous, the hunters are between us. We have to get as far away from here as we can. There are some large wooded areas nearby, we can find some shelter in those. They will not look for us there."

Kefilwe trumpeted and lumbered off towards the horizon, upon which rested a large blob that could only be the woods she had mentioned. She slowly gained speed, and for such a large animal, picked up quite a fast pace.

Kefilwe trumpeted again and Henry asked why she was doing it. She explained how she was using her call to warn the animals nearby of the approaching danger, and how her trumpeting could be heard from a long distance.

"But that is not the only sound I am making. I have a special sound called Infra-sound."

"What's inbasound?"

"In-fruh-sownd Henry, infra-sound, it carries for miles and only other elephants can hear it.

Suddenly a gazelle leaped into the air in front of them, it was instantly followed by hundreds of them, gracefully bounding like a shoal of fish leaping from the sea to escape a predatory whale. After his initial shock, Henry was astounded, they looked like a brown wave surging across the Kalahari plains. Then there were hundreds of different kinds of animal, all heading in the same direction.

Like orange lightning, Sethunya streaked past, carrying one of her cubs in her jaws, the poor thing was violently shaking from left to right as its mother surged through the grasses and the gazelles, disappearing into the dust like a ghost. In the sky, the air was thick with the calls of birds, and in places the flocks were so dense, they blocked the sun and cast shadows beneath them as would a thunder cloud.

Sethunya reappeared from the scrum of animals and hurtled towards them, this time without her cub.

"What is she doing?" he cried in alarm. "She's heading right back to the hunters!"

"She has to go back, Henry - she has to collect the rest of her cubs, but she can only carry one at a time," Kefilwe explained. "But do not worry about Sethunya, she is wise, and the fastest of us all; no hunter will get the better of her."

Kefilwe called out to her, and she slung herself round in a graceful arc and slowed to match their pace.

"How goes it Kefilwe?" she asked.

Kefilwe looked left and right, taking in the stampede.

"It looks as though we have most of us." She had a thought. "Sethunya, can you get word to Henry's family that he is safe with me? Tell them to meet us in the thick scrubs."

"Of course I can, consider it already done!"

And then, Sethunya was gone, in a flash of yellow fur and black spots.

Henry and Kefilwe were joined by more elephants; they all

gathered together on the run and formed a massive stampede of twenty and they thundered along, kicking up dust and rumbling like a thunder cloud. They all greeted each other with a chorus of trumpeting and the woods were upon them, swallowing them in its leafy mouth.

They pushed through the undergrowth, the big elephants clearing a path for the others to follow. Behind them, the procession stretched out into the savannah and out of sight. Henry wondered if this was what it looked like when all the animals went onto Noah Owl's ark thousands of years ago.

Kefilwe and the other elephants came to a halt and raised their trunks so all behind would know to stop.

"What is it?" Henry asked.

The very large bull elephant next to Kefilwe answered. His name was Mabassa.

"I think help is on its way. Listen, little owl, can you hear?"

Henry was about to inform Mabassa that he was not a Little Owl when he heard the strange ululating cry.

"Aaahh-ahaa-ah-haaaaaaaaaa-ahaah-a-haaa."

Then it repeated itself again, and again, always getting nearer. Then he saw something, something that was swinging through the trees, sometimes on branches, sometimes vines, sometimes disappearing and then reappearing.

Suddenly it thumped down onto the ground next to him. It was a human: a man; Henry shrunk back from it. Ever since he was a hatchling, Henry had been taught that humans were dangerous. However, the other animals didn't seem afraid of him. He wore just a bit of cloth around his waist and nothing more, his hair was wild and shaggy.

"Do not worry," soothed Kefilwe. "He means us no harm."

The human began to make weird babbling sounds with his mouth.

"The problem is," continued Mabassa, "no one can ever understand a word he says."

It was at this point that Henry remembered his tooth pendant. Absent mindedly, he began to stroke it with his wing tip.

"I wish we could all understand each other," he said, mainly to himself.

On cue, the tooth began to glow and buzz.

"Mumph, whumph, burble gurgle!" went the human. The human paused and looked at everyone, frustration in its face. Henry was beginning to think the magic wasn't going to work. The nearby animals all looked at each other, confused.

"Bibble babble wabble..." the human sighed – and then it happened.

"Mibbly wibbly, can you see I try to help you?"

All the animals fell silent. Kgosi, the King of the Lions strode forwards.

"How do we know we can trust you?" he demanded.

"Please, bad men come, want big white teeth!"

The strange man moved next to Kefilwe and gently stroked one of her enormous tusks.

"Big, white teeth," he repeated.

"Who are you, tell us who you are!" Kgosi ordered.

"Me Tarzowl!"

Chapter Two
Finding the Enemy

 collective gasp spread through the animals.

"He is Tarzowl!" rippled its way to the back in hushed tones. Henry leaned forwards and whispered into Kefilwe's ear.

"Who's Tarzowl?"

"He is a legend," she explained. "My father told me stories about him when I was a child, about a boy who was rescued from a wrecked plane by a family of Eagle Owls – they raised him as one of their own, and now he comes to the aid of animals in times of danger."

"Like now?" enquired Henry.

"Yes," she said. "But I thought they were just stories."

"Tarzowl, not story, Tarzowl friend!"

Kgosi leaned in close to Kefilwe.

"He is not very bright, is he?" he said.

Un-daunted, Tarzowl continued.

"You come, follow Tarzowl, we see shamans!

"What are shamans?" asked Henry.

"They are shamans!" stated Tarzowl matter of factly.

Perplexed, Henry looked at Kgosi, who just shrugged his shoulders under his mane. Tarzowl was beginning to look a bit impatient.

"Come with Tarzowl, see shamans, they know."

"I think I preferred it when I could not understand him," said Mabassa under his breath.

Those near enough to hear chortled. Tarzowl looked cross.

"Tarzowl hear!"

"Yes," said Kefilwe patiently, "We know you are here."

"No! Tarzowl HEAR!" he said, pointing at his ear to emphasise his point.

"Oh!" was Kefilwe's embarrassed reply.

There was a strained silence as the animals all looked at their feet, trying to think of something to say. An antelope shuffled her hooves in the leafy floor. Henry broke the silence first.

"I think we should trust him!" he said.

Kgosi nodded.

"It is agreed then, we go with Tarzowl, but I also think we should keep watch on the hunters. We need someone they will not be interested in." He paused as he looked for a volunteer, none was apparently forthcoming.

"I'll do it," chimed Henry.

Kefilwe began to protest.

"Oh, well, now, I am not so sure about that, I promised to keep you safe."

"Yes but, I'm small…"

"I know, but…"

"And I'm silent when I fly…"

"I know, but…"

"And I don't have big white teeth."

"Little owl right!" blurted Tarzowl. "Bad men want big white teeth and fur and skin." To emphasise his point he gently ran his hand through Kgosi's thick mane. Kgosi growled quietly and then made his decision.

"Very well, Henry, you will spy on the hunters…but do you know where they are camped?"

Henry's enthusiasm slipped a little, this was an unexpected stumbling block.

"Oh! No, I don't."

A small dark brown bird hopped down from a nearby rhino, it had a yellow beak.

"I know the way, I know the way!" it chirruped joyfully, twitching and bobbing its head around, constantly on the lookout for nearby edible bugs. "I am Tatenda, I know where they are, follow me, follow me!"

Tatenda is an ox pecker, a bird that lives on the backs of plains animals like rhino, elephants and bison, where it feeds on irritating flies and skin parasites. Kgosi chuckled.

"It seems you have found your guide," the Lion King declared.

"Be careful," said Kefilwe.

It was clear that Tatenda was eager to be off,. So too was Henry. Tatenda was hard to follow through the undergrowth; he kept on disappearing for short periods, then re-appearing, agitated that Henry was struggling to keep up. Quickly, they reached the edge of the woodlands, and once more Henry was hit by the heat of the savannah; he'd got used to the cool of the woodland shade.

Out in the open, Tatenda was a lot easier to follow. Flying low to the grasses they were impossible to detect, and shortly their quarry drew into view. Up ahead there were some tents, surrounded by a thick wall of sharp spiny branches that had been cut down and arranged into a defensive circle to keep out predators. Despite all of their machinery and weapons, humans are very weak animals. Overhanging the camp was an enormous acacia tree. Henry and Tatenda flitted their way to the topmost branch and perched there, where they could observe the enemy from safety.

Chapter Three
A Close Shave

 ndetected, Henry and Tatenda watched at their leisure. They had discovered a group of three men, who were sat at a cramped table studying a mess of maps. There was rubbish everywhere: food wrappers; empty plastic bottles; tins – the amount of filth these men had brought with them - and were living in - was disgusting! The men wore wide floppy hats to keep their heads cool, their khaki-coloured short-sleeve shirts were soaked in sweat as they baked in the heat of the sun, and they smelt horrible – like socks that had been worn for a hundred years and never washed. Henry

couldn't see their faces, but he imagined that they didn't look very nice. One of them stood, stretched and arched his back, making all his bones pop and crackle like bursting bubble wrap; his name was Phillip StJohn Smythe, he was the first to speak.

"Good hunt this morning eh chaps?"

The others nodded in agreement. One of the others, a man called Bertrand, replied. He had a French accent.

"Yes, zees skins should bring us a good few souzand dollaers!" he continued. "What eez for tomorrow Philleep?"

"The ivory!" Phillip replied, then he paused for thought before carrying on. "Look here." He began pointing at one of the maps. "We have four large herds, one here, one here, and two here."

The third man, Parrington piped up and in turn began pointing at the map.

"I have teams of chasers set up near the herds, we drive them through these routes," he said, tracing his finger along the paper. "And get them to converge into this valley and force them off this cliff edge. Then we collect the ivory at our leisure."

Phillip pulled his hat off to reveal an unsightly bald head that was gooey with thick globules of sticky sweat. He wiped it away with a grotty red handkerchief and then proceeded to scratch his freckled scalp. Parrington removed his hat too; his head was covered in close-cropped red hair. He had a sharp pinched up sort of face and lots of thick stubble.

"What about the wardens? We don't want them on our tails."

Phillip sniggered.

"Don't worry about those idiots, they are already too busy chasing around after small-time pet traders!"

"But how do you know?" asked Bertrand.

"Because I organised and planted them!" crowed Phillip. "Don't worry, if there are any wardens, they are miles away – we will have this reserve to ourselves."

These men were scary, and that is just what Henry was feeling right now. He was also very angry about the men's plan to hurt the elephants.

"What's a reserve?" he asked of Tatenda.

"All of this place is," he replied, "This reserve is where all the animals are supposed to be able to live in safety away from sick people like these who just want to kill everything."

"What is ivory?" Henry asked.

Tatenda had to stop for a moment to think, and then he caught up with himself.

"Ivory, Henry, is what is in elephant tusks – their 'Big white teeth' as Tarzowl would say."

Henry was mortified!

"What on earth would people want with elephant tusks? It's not as if they need them to eat with."

"No, Henry, it is worse. They take the tusks to people who strip them down and then carve them into useless trinkets and nick-nacks."

"That's ridiculous!"

"No Henry, this is ridiculous, some people believe things like tusks and rhino horn have magical healing things about them, but they do not; tusks are just teeth, and rhino horn is nothing more than one big thick piece of hair, similar to your claws."

Henry inspected his feet.

"Well there's nothing magical about my claws."

"And neither is there anything magical about tusks and rhino horn, it is just stupid humans and their silly beliefs!"

Henry and Tatenda were dragged from their discussion by Phillip.

"Tomorrow at dawn then! So, who's for a spot of hunting before we turn in?"

Parrington and Bertrand each reached under the table and pulled out a rifle. Parrington patted the stock of his rifle, and stroked the barrel lovingly.

"It looks like we are already ready." Mused Bertrand.

"Let's try our luck in the woods over there, you never know what you might find in the undergrowth." exclaimed Phillip.

Henry gasped in sudden realisation. The woods the man had indicated were the ones where his and Tatenda's friends were secretly hiding away in from these men.

"Oh no!" he exclaimed. "Tatenda, everyone's in danger, we've got to warn them!"

Tatenda agreed, and of they flew, exactly at the same moment that Phillip looked up at their tree. He saw them!

"By golly!" he exclaimed. "It's a bally snowy owl, what's it doing all the way out here, and in the day time?"

His companions also looked to see for themselves.

"What is it doing with an ox pecker? It looks like they are having a conversation with each other!"

"Whatever!" said Parrington dismissively, "It looks like we have our first sport!"

He took aim with his rifle and squeezed off a round.

CRACK

The noise was deafening.

Thankfully his aim was slow and he missed, but his shot was close enough to send a shockwave of air over the backs of Henry and Tatenda.

"Dive!" shouted Tatenda. "If we skim low enough through the grasses and scrub, they will never hit us, just dodge and weave like me."

Henry only needed telling once; he had never been shot at before! The grass tips whipped at his feet and stung like nettles, so he tucked them into his deep coat of feathers. Twisting and turning, Tatenda and Henry zipped closer to the forest edge as another bullet sang harmlessly overhead and made a branch from a tree they were passing explode into splinters. Sensing they were now out of harm's way, they slowed their pace to catch their breaths, and finally reached the dark safety of the forest once more. They landed roughly on the soft, leafy ground.

"Phew!" Henry exhaled, "That was too close!"

Chapter 4
The Plan is Made

When Henry and Tatenda returned to the clearing, the amount of animals gathered there had tripled. It took them ages to fly back to Kefilwe, Kgosi and Mabassa; Tarzowl was still there too. The forest was thick with the sound of worried animal voices, and here and there was the occasional crying of a youngster.

Henry's friends listened intently as he and Tatenda recounted their findings, and the rest of the animals waited in silence as Kgosi made his decision.

"That settles it!" he said.

His words would have had more impact had a nearby young elephant not chosen that moment to punctuate Kgosi's drama with an enormously loud fart!

PHWAAARRRRP

Mabassa shot a vicious glance at the young culprit, who didn't seem to care in the slightest anyway, and just continued to munch noisily away on leafy twigs from overhead.

Kgosi continued.

"As I was saying, we have to go to the shamans. If we can barely understand Tarzowl, we should have a good chance with them."

Henry had an idea.

"Hey, guys! Listen! Why don't we do two things at the same time? Kgosi, I have a plan!"

Henry drew out what he could remember of the map on the sandy dusty floor with a stick in his beak. He explained how the hunters planned to approach their clearing through the valley.

"This is the clever bit!" he finished in triumph. "Here is where we dig a big trap in the ground and cover it, and we trap them!" He stabbed at the middle of the valley.

"This is a good idea, but none of us are good at digging," responded Kgosi.

"We are!" said a strange little voice from the floor. Everyone looked for the owner. Tatenda spotted the source; it was a naked mole rat. It looked like a rat with no hair – pink and with small eyes. Kgosi couldn't believe what he saw.

"How can you be of help? We need an enormous hole big enough to hold their metal monster that carries them around."

The mole rat was not to be put off.

"We live underground and dig our own tunnels and homes right where they will come through. We can easily dig a great big hole out of all our tunnels - there are thousands of us. We can dig right up to under the surface; no one but us will know."

It couldn't go wrong; the plan was fool-proof. Henry suggested that Kgosi go with Tarzowl to the shamans; he thought it best that they get the shamans to alert the reserve keepers and let them know where the poachers were going to be found.

Henry and Tatenda flew out to where they had been told the mole rats lived to watch as they excavated. The rest of the animals remained in hiding in the undergrowth.

Back in the sun they arrived to find there were already substantial piles of earth all around. This immediately caused alarm, the idea of a trap is that the trap is not obvious. But the elephants nearby had already thought of that. A herd of them stomped up, carefully avoiding the edges of the massive hole growing underground – it was marked out by a square ring of older rats, too frail to dig so fast. The elephants were busy sweeping the piles of earth away as they appeared, and some were blowing away what they had not been able to collect with their trunks. Soon enough, the piles of earth had stopped appearing and the trap was set. The animals scattered and hid.

Henry carefully hopped across the trap to meet the head of the mole rats, who assured him it was a very deep hole indeed – big enough to stop the men. All that remained was to creep out of sight and wait.

The wait did not last long. The sound of an approaching jeep faded into earshot, sounding like a whining and groaning as it bumped over grassy hillocks and bumped over sharp rocks and stones. Then it heaved into view – right on-track for the trap underground. The jeep pulled up just shy of the trap edge – oh no! Just one more foot along the way and it would have crashed through the thin cover of the hole. The driver St. John killed the engine and looked around. Parrington declared this would do as a point to walk from.

"Don't want to scare off the game!"

The other men nodded and exited the vehicle. They were in the process of removing their rifles when the sound of another motor vehicle dissolved into existence.

The men looked at each other; fear was clear to see in their eyes.

"Oh, no, what shall we do!?" demanded Parrington.

St John Smythe wasted no time.

"Quick, jump back in and get us out of here, it's the rangers, go, go, go, go, go, go!"

The jeep roared into life, all four wheels shooting up plumes of dust at it wheel spun away – right across the mole rat's huge trap. KAWHUMPF! It took a while for the dense cloud of dust to clear. When it did, the jeep had disappeared. In its place was a huge hole, the jeep was silent, all that could be heard was the coughing and splattering of the three bad men.

Approaching from the north were three jeeps carrying a number of African rangers, some armed with hunting rifles. They all stopped at the hole and got out. Looking in the trap, the animal loving keepers saw three very dusty and angry hunters and poachers. The rangers were scratching their heads in bemusement and could not understand just how this had happened. Wasting no time they pointed their rifles at the men and after

helping them out with ropes, they arrested them, placed them in hand cuffs and took them away.

"Hooray, the bad men are gone!" cheered Tatenda. "Come on, Henry, let us go tell the others the good news!"

So, back to the clearing in the woods they went for the last time and spread the word.

"Henry Owl!"

It was Mum!

Henry turned around – his family had been brought to the hiding place. What to do? What to say?

"Um I can explain mummy, daddy..."

"No need, son," said a proud Daddy Owl. "We have been told all about it on the way here, about a brave little owl who has saved the day, so here we are – it could only have been you."

"Well, I had a lot of help," said Henry modestly.

"Yes, but the ideas were yours!" Kgosi cheered.

The ivory poachers were never seen or heard from again.

The End

Acknowledgements

Thank you to everyone in my life who has encouraged me, helped me and supported me in the last twelve to eighteen months – you all know who you are, and how much I love you; if it weren't for you, well…

Thank you to all the VERY FEW teachers in my life who taught and inspired and believed in me, thank you to the majority of the teachers in my life who taught me how NOT to be a teacher.

Thank you to my friends, my family, Harriet, Henry and Lily - my darling children (when they want to be or when there's money to be had), you guys are my everything.

Thank you to Jon and Corinna my Editors and publisher, for reading this so many times over and for making it happen.

Thank you Mum for screaming me into this world and your words of encouragement. Thank you for all your sacrifices and a lifetime of love. I'm so not sorry for covering your kitchen table with ants when I was five, or sorry for filling the house with bugs. I haven't yet decided if I'm sorry for when I had a wee in the hoover pipe when I was six and blamed it on Jen, um, yes, that was me! I'm sure it was all worth it. Oh and it was me that smashed the front room window at Clouds Hill Road. I hit it with one of dad's golf balls. It wasn't Jenny at all. Too late to stop my pocket money now! I luvs you are Muhh!

Thanks Dad for showing me how to use tools and do funky stuff to houses. As a kid I hated not being paid to help you with your DIY and fitting windows, as a man I value and cherish the skills you passed on to me to practice and hone. Thank you for the lost time we have been making up these recent years – I love you dad. Thank you for telling and encouraging me to write down the stories I told the kids all those times I put them to bed over the years – I have finally listened to you, but don't expect me to change a habit of a lifetime overnight okay? Remember – without education, PVC wouldn't have been invented!

Thank you Edna and Jeff for trying the best you could. It was so hard for you as step parents. There is no manual to equip us for this, it's like giving birth to a teenager and we have all taken lessons from our experiences in this situation. I know I have. As an almost step parent myself I understand the challenges and difficulties it brings.

Thanks, Nan and Poppa, Nanny and Grandad – I miss you all so much and will always carry my happy childhood memories of all of your love in my heart and strive to be ever as loving to all my children (paternal origin and the three I bought off eBay) and their children in turn and break their hearts when I leave for the great authors' writing room in the sky one day.

To my sister Jen – I'm not sorry for anything, you deserved everything you got! You so deserved suffocation for crying when I was trying to watch Rainbow! Love you really, thank you for supporting me in the dark times, and thank you for being my sister – someone had to and thank you for my lovely niece and nephews (Thanks for sorting her out Bunny mon Bro)!

To my sister Maddy – took your time! To be fair though, you have been coping with me moaning about where the illustrations are as well as dealing with my gorgeous little niece Jessica Owl, and poorly wrists. And there's me (yes I started a sentence with "and") thinking you girls can multi-task…However, I'm still not sorry for holding you upside down by your ankles and shouting at you to go to bed when I used to baby sit you when our parents went out.

A special thank you to Harriet for assisting in the editing of this book, note I did all the hard work and you just spotted the mistakes I made when typing under the influence of sauvingnon blanc. Enjoy spending your first professional editing commission.

Thank you to Stu and Rich for all the fun we had in our youth. Sorry Rich for putting in your wedding card about the time you did a poo and wee off the 200 foot high Shepton Mallet viaduct. Oops now thousands of people know about it…You were just as bad Stu!

Thank you to Lisa, the special woman in my life who has shown me my true self after so so many years of self-doubt. I love you. Thanks Brook, Eliana and Louis – I love you guys too.

Thank you to each and every one of my amazing Bugfest team – for your support, honesty, loyalty and love; I literally couldn't have made it without you.

If there is anyone else I have forgotten to mention, I'm sure you have some sort of relevance or importance, just count yourself amongst everyone at the top.

About the Author

Nick was born in 1973 and from the time he could first walk he has always been fascinated with nature. He grew up in the countryside and the love he has for all things non-human has never waned. He is a teacher and teacher trainer and has worked as a professional children's entertainer and wildlife show presenter for a number of years; he is always desperate for attention.

He lives in Weymouth, Dorset and enjoys looking out across the bay from his writing desk in the attic room where he daydreams make believe worlds and people. Some think he is a bit eccentric, and he would agree, and happily states he'd "rather be eccentric than boring like a lot of other people." He tries very hard not to be cynical, but sometimes cynicism gets the better of him despite his attempts to look at the world through rose tinted glasses.

He can often be seen hiding under the peddle boats waiting to pounce on and terrify the passing seagulls who have got far too big for their boots – well, who else is going to put them back in their place? Sometimes he gets it wrong and shocks sweet little old grannies – last week, one had to be taken to hospital for emergency surgery because he made her swallow her false teeth.

STILL ON THE TRACK OF UNKNOWN ANIMALS

T he Centre for Fortean Zoology, or CFZ, is a non profit-making organisation founded in 1992 with the aim of being a clearing house for information, and coordinating research into mystery animals around the world.

We also study out of place animals, rare and aberrant animal behaviour, and Zooform Phenomena; little-understood "things" that appear to be animals, but which are in fact nothing of the sort, and not even alive (at least in the way we understand the term).

Not only are we the biggest organisation of our type in the world, but - or so we like to think - we are the best. We are certainly the only truly global cryptozoological research organisation, and we carry out our investigations using a strictly scientific set of guidelines. We are expanding all the time and looking to recruit new members to help us in our research into mysterious animals and strange creatures across the globe.

Why should you join us? Because, if you are genuinely interested in trying to solve the last great mysteries of Mother Nature, there is nobody better than us with whom to do it.

Members get a four-issue subscription to our journal *Animals & Men.* Each issue contains nearly 100 pages packed with news, articles, letters, research papers, field reports, and even a gossip column! The magazine is Royal Octavo in format with a full colour cover. You also have access to one of the world's largest collections of resource material dealing with cryptozoology and allied disciplines, and people from the CFZ membership regularly take part in fieldwork and expeditions around the world.

The CFZ is managed by a three-man board of trustees, with a non-profit making trust registered with HM Government Stamp Office. The board of trustees is supported by a Permanent Directorate of full and part-time staff, and advised by a Consultancy Board of specialists - many of whom are world-renowned experts in their particular field. We have regional representatives across the UK, the USA, and many other parts of the world, and are affiliated with

You'll find that the people at the CFZ are friendly and approachable. We have a thriving forum on the website which is the hub of an ever-growing electronic community. You will soon find your feet. Many members of the CFZ Permanent Directorate started off as ordinary members, and now work full-time chasing monsters around the world.

Write to us, e-mail us, or telephone us. The list of future projects on the website is not exhaustive. If you have a good idea for an investigation, please tell us. We may well be able to help.

We are always looking for volunteers to join us. If you see a project that interests you, do not hesitate to get in touch with us. Under certain circumstances we can help provide funding for your trip. If you look on the future projects section of the website, you can see some of the projects that we have pencilled in for the next few years.

In 2003 and 2004 we sent three-man expeditions to Sumatra looking for Orang-Pendek - a semi-legendary bipedal ape. The same three went to Mongolia in 2005. All three members started off merely subscribers to the CFZ magazine. Next time it could be you!

We have no magic sources of income. All our funds come from donations, membership fees, and sales of our publications and merchandise. We are always looking for corporate sponsorship, and other sources of revenue. If you have any ideas for fund-raising please let us know. However, unlike other cryptozoological organisations in the past, we do not live in an intellectual ivory tower. We are not afraid to get our hands dirty, and furthermore we are not one of those organisations where the membership have to raise money so that a privileged few can go on expensive foreign trips. Our research teams, both in the UK and abroad, consist of a mixture of experienced and inexperienced personnel. We are truly a community, and work on the premise that the benefits of CFZ membership are open to all.

Reports of our investigations are published on our website as soon as they are available. Preliminary reports are posted within days of the project finishing.

Each year we publish a 200 page yearbook

We have a thriving YouTube channel, CFZtv, which has well over two hundred self-made documentaries, lecture appearances, and episodes of our monthly webTV show. We have a daily online magazine, which has over a million hits each year.

Each year since 2000 we have held our annual convention - the Weird Weekend. It is three days of lectures, workshops, and excursions. But most importantly it is a chance for members of the CFZ to meet each other, and to talk with the members of the permanent directorate in a relaxed and informal setting and preferably with a pint of beer in one hand. Since 2006 - the Weird Weekend has been bigger and better and held on the third weekend in August in the idyllic rural location of Woolsery in North Devon.

Since relocating to North Devon in 2005 we have become ever more closely involved with other community organisations, and we hope that this trend will continue. We have also worked closely with Police Forces across the UK as consultants for animal mutilation cases, and we intend to forge closer links with the coastguard and other community services. We want to work closely with those who regularly travel into the Bristol Channel, so that if the recent trend of exotic animal visitors to our coastal waters continues, we can be out there as soon as possible.

Apart from having been the only Fortean Zoological organisation in the world to have consistently published material on all aspects of the subject for over a decade, we have achieved the following concrete results:

• Disproved the myth relating to the headless so-called sea-serpent carcass of Durgan beach in Cornwall 1975

• Disproved the story

of the 1988 puma skull of Lustleigh Cleave

- Carried out the only in-depth research ever into the mythos of the Cornish Owlman.
- Made the first records of a tropical species of lamprey
- Made the first records of a luminous cave gnat larva in Thailand
- Discovered a possible new species of British mammal - the beech marten
- In 1994-6 carried out the first archival fortean zoological survey of Hong Kong
- In the year 2000, CFZ theories were confirmed when a new species of lizard was added to the British List
- Identified the monster of Martin Mere in Lancashire as a giant wels catfish
- Expanded the known range of Armitage's skink in the Gambia by 80%
- Obtained photographic evidence of the remains of Europe's largest known pike
- Carried out the first ever in-depth study of the ninki-nanka
- Carried out the first attempt to breed Puerto Rican cave snails in captivity
- Were the first European explorers to visit the `lost valley` in Sumatra
- Published the first ever evidence for a new tribe of pygmies in Guyana
- Published the first evidence for a new species of caiman in Guyana

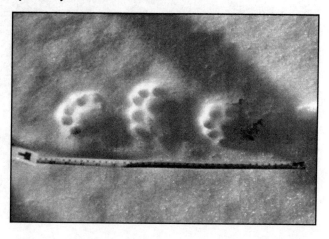

on a monster-haunted lake in Ireland for the first time
- Had a sighting of orang pendek in Sumatra in 2009
- Found leopard hair, subsequently identified by DNA analysis, from rural North Devon in 2010
- Brought back hairs which appear to be from an unknown primate in Sumatra
- Published some of the best evidence ever for the almasty in southern Russia

CFZ Expeditions and Investigations include:

- 1998 Puerto Rico, Florida, Mexico (Chupacabras)
- 1999 Nevada (Bigfoot)
- 2000 Thailand (Naga)
- 2002 Martin Mere (Giant catfish)
- 2002 Cleveland (Wallaby mutilation)
- 2003 Bolam Lake (BHM Reports)

- 2003 Sumatra (Orang Pendek)
- 2003 Texas (Bigfoot; giant snapping turtles)
- 2004 Sumatra (Orang Pendek; cigau, a sabre-toothed cat)
- 2004 Illinois (Black panthers; cicada swarm)
- 2004 Texas (Mystery blue dog)
- Loch Morar (Monster)
- 2004 Puerto Rico (Chupacabras; carnivorous cave snails)
- 2005 Belize (Affiliate expedition for hairy dwarfs)
- 2005 Loch Ness (Monster)
- 2005 Mongolia (Allghoi Khorkhoi aka Mongolian death worm)

- 2006 Gambia (Gambo - Gambian sea monster , Ninki Nanka and Armitage's skink
- 2006 Llangorse Lake (Giant pike, giant eels)
- 2006 Windermere (Giant eels)
- 2007 Coniston Water (Giant eels)
- 2007 Guyana (Giant anaconda, didi, water tiger)
- 2008 Russia (Almasty)
- 2009 Sumatra (Orang pendek)
- 2009 Republic of Ireland (Lake Monster)
- 2010 Texas (Blue Dogs)
- 2010 India (Mande Burung)
- 2011 Sumatra (Orang-pendek)

For details of current membership fees, current expeditions and investigations, and voluntary posts within the CFZ that need your help, please do not hesitate to contact us.

The Centre for Fortean Zoology,
Myrtle Cottage,
Woolfardisworthy,
Bideford, North Devon
EX39 5QR

Telephone 01237 431413
Fax+44 (0)7006-074-925
eMail info@cfz.org.uk

Websites:

www.cfz.org.uk
www.weirdweekend.org

THE WORLD'S WEIRDEST PUBLISHING COMPANY

HOW TO START A PUBLISHING EMPIRE

Unlike most mainstream publishers, we have a non-commercial remit, and our mission state-
ment claims that "we publish books because they deserve to be published, not because we
think that we can make money out of them". Our motto is the Latin Tag *Pro bona causa
facimus* (we do it for good reason), a slogan taken from a children's book *The Case of the Sil-
ver Egg* by the late Desmond Skirrow.

WIKIPEDIA: "The first book published was in 1988. *Take this Brother may it Serve
you Well* was a guide to Beatles bootlegs by Jonathan Downes. It sold quite well, but
was hampered by very poor production values, being photocopied, and held together
by a plastic clip binder. In 1988 A5 clip binders were hard to get hold of, so the publishers took A4 binders and cut them in half with a hacksaw. It now reaches surpris-
ingly high prices second hand.

The production quality improved slightly over the years, and after 1999 all the books
produced were ringbound with laminated colour covers. In 2004, however, they
signed an agreement with Lightning Source, and all books are now produced perfect
bound, with full colour covers."

Until 2010 all our books, the majority of which are/were on the subject of mystery animals
and allied disciplines, were published by `CFZ Press`, the publishing arm of the Centre for
Fortean Zoology (CFZ), and we urged our readers and followers to draw a discreet veil over
the books that we published that were completely off topic to the CFZ.

However, in 2010 we decided that enough was enough and launched a second imprint,
`Fortean Words` which aims to cover a wide range of non animal-related esoteric subjects.
Other imprints will be launched as and when we feel like it, however the basic ethos of the
company remains the same: Our job is to publish books and magazines that we feel are worth
publishing, whether or not they are going to sell. Money is, after all - as my dear old Mama
once told me - a rather vulgar subject, and she would be rolling in her grave if she thought that
her eldest son was somehow in `trade`.

Luckily, so far our tastes have turned out not
to be that rarified after all, and we have sold
far more books than anyone ever thought that
we would, so there is a moral in there somewhere…

Jon Downes,
Woolsery, North Devon
July 2010

CFZ PRESS

Other Books in Print

Wildman! by Redfern, Nick
Globsters by Newton, Michael
Cats of Magic, Mythology and Mystery Shuker, by Karl P. N
Those Amazing Newfoundland Dogs by Bondeson, Jan
The Mystery Animals of Pennsylvania by Gable, Andrew
Sea Serpent Carcasses - Scotland from the Stronsa Monster to Loch Ness by Glen Vaudrey
The CFZ Yearbook 2012 edited by Jonathan and Corinna Downes
ORANG PENDEK: Sumatra's Forgotten Ape by Richard Freeman
THE MYSTERY ANIMALS OF THE BRITISH ISLES: London by Neil Arnold
CFZ EXPEDITION REPORT: India 2010 by Richard Freeman *et al*
The Cryptid Creatures of Florida by Scott Marlow
Dead of Night by Lee Walker
The Mystery Animals of the British Isles: The Northern Isles by Glen Vaudrey
THE MYSTERY ANIMALS OF THE BRTISH ISLES: Gloucestershire and Worcestershire by Paul Williams
When Bigfoot Attacks by Michael Newton
Weird Waters – The Mystery Animals of Scandinavia: Lake and Sea Monsters by Lars Thomas
The Inhumanoids by Barton Nunnelly
Monstrum! A Wizard's Tale by Tony "Doc" Shiels
CFZ Yearbook 2011 edited by Jonathan Downes
Karl Shuker's Alien Zoo by Shuker, Dr Karl P.N
Tetrapod Zoology Book One by Naish, Dr Darren
The Mystery Animals of Ireland by Gary Cunningham and Ronan Coghlan
Monsters of Texas by Gerhard, Ken
The Great Yokai Encyclopaedia by Freeman, Richard
NEW HORIZONS: Animals & Men issues 16-20 Collected Editions Vol. 4 by Downes, Jonathan
A Daintree Diary -
Tales from Travels to the Daintree Rainforest in tropical north Queensland, Australia by Portman, Carl
Strangely Strange but Oddly Normal by Roberts, Andy

Centre for Fortean Zoology Yearbook 2010 by Downes, Jonathan
Predator Deathmatch by Molloy, Nick
Star Steeds and other Dreams by Shuker, Karl
CHINA: A Yellow Peril? by Muirhead, Richard
Mystery Animals of the British Isles: The Western Isles by Vaudrey, Glen
Giant Snakes - Unravelling the coils of mystery by Newton, Michael
Mystery Animals of the British Isles: Kent by Arnold, Neil
Centre for Fortean Zoology Yearbook 2009 by Downes, Jonathan
CFZ EXPEDITION REPORT: Russia 2008 by Richard Freeman *et al*, Shuker, Karl (fwd)
Dinosaurs and other Prehistoric Animals on Stamps - A Worldwide catalogue
by Shuker, Karl P. N
Dr Shuker's Casebook by Shuker, Karl P.N
The Island of Paradise - chupacabra UFO crash retrievals,
and accelerated evolution on the island of Puerto Rico by Downes, Jonathan
The Mystery Animals of the British Isles: Northumberland and Tyneside by Hallowell, Michael J
Centre for Fortean Zoology Yearbook 1997 by Downes, Jonathan (Ed)
Centre for Fortean Zoology Yearbook 2002 by Downes, Jonathan (Ed)
Centre for Fortean Zoology Yearbook 2000/1 by Downes, Jonathan (Ed)
Centre for Fortean Zoology Yearbook 1998 by Downes, Jonathan (Ed)
Centre for Fortean Zoology Yearbook 2003 by Downes, Jonathan (Ed)
In the wake of Bernard Heuvelmans by Woodley, Michael A
CFZ EXPEDITION REPORT: Guyana 2007 by Richard Freeman *et al*, Shuker, Karl (fwd)
Centre for Fortean Zoology Yearbook 1999 by Downes, Jonathan (Ed)
Big Cats in Britain Yearbook 2008 by Fraser, Mark (Ed)
Centre for Fortean Zoology Yearbook 1996 by Downes, Jonathan (Ed)
THE CALL OF THE WILD - Animals & Men issues 11-15
Collected Editions Vol. 3 by Downes, Jonathan (ed)
Ethna's Journal by Downes, C N
Centre for Fortean Zoology Yearbook 2008 by Downes, J (Ed)
DARK DORSET -Calendar Custome by Newland, Robert J
Extraordinary Animals Revisited by Shuker, Karl
MAN-MONKEY - In Search of the British Bigfoot by Redfern, Nick
Dark Dorset Tales of Mystery, Wonder and Terror by Newland, Robert J and Mark North
Big Cats Loose in Britain by Matthews, Marcus
MONSTER! - The A-Z of Zooform Phenomena by Arnold, Neil
The Centre for Fortean Zoology 2004 Yearbook by Downes, Jonathan (Ed)
The Centre for Fortean Zoology 2007 Yearbook by Downes, Jonathan (Ed)
CAT FLAPS! Northern Mystery Cats by Roberts, Andy
Big Cats in Britain Yearbook 2007 by Fraser, Mark (Ed)
BIG BIRD! - Modern sightings of Flying Monsters by Gerhard, Ken
THE NUMBER OF THE BEAST - Animals & Men issues 6-10
Collected Editions Vol. 1 by Downes, Jonathan (Ed)
IN THE BEGINNING - Animals & Men issues 1-5 Collected Editions Vol. 1 by Downes, Jonathan
STRENGTH THROUGH KOI - They saved Hitler's Koi and other stories

by Downes, Jonathan
The Smaller Mystery Carnivores of the Westcountry by Downes, Jonathan
CFZ EXPEDITION REPORT: Gambia 2006 by Richard Freeman *et al*, Shuker, Karl (fwd)
The Owlman and Others by Jonathan Downes
The Blackdown Mystery by Downes, Jonathan
Big Cats in Britain Yearbook 2006 by Fraser, Mark (Ed)
Fragrant Harbours - Distant Rivers by Downes, John T
Only Fools and Goatsuckers by Downes, Jonathan
Monster of the Mere by Jonathan Downes
Dragons:More than a Myth by Freeman, Richard Alan
Granfer's Bible Stories by Downes, John Tweddell
Monster Hunter by Downes, Jonathan

CFZ Classics is a new venture for us. There are many seminal works that are either unavailable today, or not available with the production values which we would like to see. So, following the old adage that if you want to get something done do it yourself, this is exactly what we have done.

Desiderius Erasmus Roterodamus (b. October 18th 1466, d. July 2nd 1536) said: "When I have a little money, I buy books; and if I have any left, I buy food and clothes," and we are much the same. Only, we are in the lucky position of being able to share our books with the wider world. CFZ Classics is a conduit through which we cannot just re-issue titles which we feel still have much to offer the cryptozoological and Fortean research communities of the 21st Century, but we are adding footnotes, supplementary essays, and other material where we deem it appropriate.

Headhunters of The Amazon by Fritz W Up de Graff (1902)

Fortean Words

The Centre for Fortean Zoology has for several years led the field in Fortean publishing. CFZ Press is the only publishing company specialising in books on monsters and mystery animals. CFZ Press has published more books on this subject than any other company in history and has attracted such well known authors as Andy Roberts, Nick Redfern, Michael Newton, Dr Karl Shuker, Neil Arnold, Dr Darren Naish, Jon Downes, Ken Gerhard and Richard Freeman.

Now CFZ Press are launching a new imprint. Fortean Words is a new line of books dealing with Fortean subjects other than cryptozoology, which is - after all - the subject the CFZ are best known for. Fortean Words is being launched with a spectacular multi-volume series called *Haunted Skies* which covers British UFO sightings between 1940 and 2010. Former policeman John Hanson and his long-suffering partner Dawn Holloway have compiled a peerless library of sighting reports, many that have not been made public before.

Other books include a look at the Berwyn Mountains UFO case by renowned Fortean Andy Roberts and a series of forthcoming books by transatlantic researcher Nick Redfern. CFZ Press are dedicated to maintaining the fine quality of their works with Fortean Words. New authors tackling new subjects will always be encouraged, and we hope that our books will continue to be as ground-breaking and popular as ever.

Haunted Skies Volume One 1940-1959 by John Hanson and Dawn Holloway
Haunted Skies Volume Two 1960-1965 by John Hanson and Dawn Holloway
Haunted Skies Volume Three 1965-1967 by John Hanson and Dawn Holloway
Haunted Skies Volume Four 1968-1971 by John Hanson and Dawn Holloway
Haunted Skies Volume Five 1972-1974 by John Hanson and Dawn Holloway
Haunted Skies Volume Six 1975-1977 by John Hanson and Dawn Holloway
Grave Concerns by Kai Roberts

Police and the Paranormal by Andy Owens
Dead of Night by Lee Walker
Space Girl Dead on Spaghetti Junction - an anthology by Nick Redfern
I Fort the Lore - an anthology by Paul Screeton
UFO Down - the Berwyn Mountains UFO Crash by Andy Roberts
The Grail by Ronan Coghlan
UFO Warminster - Cradle of Contract by Kevin Goodman
Quest for the Hexham Heads by Paul Screeton

Fortean Fiction

J ust before Christmas 2011, we launched our third imprint, this time dedicated to - let's see if you guessed it from the title - fictional books with a Fortean or cryptozoological theme. We have published a few fictional books in the past, but now think that because of our rising reputation as publishers of quality Forteana, that a dedicated fiction imprint was the order of the day.

We launched with four titles:

Green Unpleasant Land by Richard Freeman
Left Behind by Harriet Wadham
Dark Ness by Tabitca Cope
Snap! By Steven Bredice
Death on Dartmoor by Di Francis
Dark Wear by Tabitca Cope
Hyakymonogatari Book 1 by Richard Freeman

Lightning Source UK Ltd.
Milton Keynes UK
UKOW05f2241040714

234592UK00001B/1/P